SAVING ZANE

KACI ROSE

CONTENTS

GET FREE BOOKS!

CHAPTER 1

ZANE

Watching people's mouths move but not being able to hear a word of it is a very odd sensation. Sometimes they just try to speak louder and over pronounce their words, thinking that maybe I'll be able to read their lips but I can't.

Until a few weeks ago, I had my hearing. Then, one bombing later, not only do I have scars and PTSD, but worse, my world has gone completely silent.

Though I've gotten some sick entertainment by watching people give up trying to get me to understand them and finally write what they have to say. I've got to say, this nurse is smart. She pulls out her phone and uses the text to speech before turning it around to let me read it.

Later today, they will be here to transport you to Oakside. They've got someone there who will teach you sign language. Your doctor visits and physical therapy will all be on site. Do you have any questions?

Shaking my head no seems to satisfy her. I guess handing me a pamphlet on Oakside is easier than trying to explain it to someone who can't hear you.

The place looks interesting. Kind of like a fancy bed-and-breakfast for healing injured military personnel. I have to say the food promised to be a hell of a lot better than the barely identifiable meat substance I was given for lunch today.

As I wait for them to come in and get me, I look over the pamphlet again. When the nurse finally shows up, she insists on pushing me down in a wheelchair with all my stuff in my lap. A long time ago, I learned not to fight them on things like this. It was easier to just climb into the wheelchair and let them take me wherever we're going.

The ride over to Oakside is fairly easy, and it's nice to see something other than the walls of a hospital.

At least once I get to Oakside, they're not insisting on a wheelchair anymore. Why they were doing it the first place is a mystery. Though I can't hear, I can see just fine.

After driving down a tree-lined driveway, we arrive at the large Plantation-style building at the Oakside. Outside, ready to greet me is a man with a bunch of scars with a beautiful blonde by his side. Greeting me, he smiles, handing me a piece of paper.

I'm Noah and this is my wife, Lexi. We run Oakside and we'll be showing you to your room. Let us know if, at any point, you need anything. We've supplied your room with a whiteboard, washable markers, plenty of pads, paper, pens, and journals.

Nodding, I smile. I haven't tried to talk since losing my hearing. I figure there's no point in it. Who knows if they'll even be able to understand me?

After they show me to my room, they aren't gone more than a minute before another couple is at my door.

This one's holding a tablet and hands it to me to read.

I'm Faith and this is Logan, my fiancé. Logan was a patient here and had lost his voice. I taught him ASL and different tricks to communicate with the outside world. That's what I am here to teach you as well.

This tablet is yours. I figure it's probably easier to communicate this way than writing on a whiteboard or paper all the time. At least Logan thought so. I will give you a few days to settle in, and we will start on Monday.

Once again, I gave her a nod and a small smile. This seems to appease her and they both leave the room.

At least the people here at Oakside seem pretty chipper and appear to be go-getters. Hopefully, that translates into my healing process as well.

Not that anything's really going to help. It's not as if I'll miraculously be able to hear again or have my life back. Not that I have much to live for, anyway. The Navy SEALs were my whole life, and before this blast they were trying to convince me to retire at the ripe old age of thirty-nine.

Even now at thirty-five, I have no idea what I wanted to do with the rest of my life. I always thought that the SEALs were my game plan. I don't have anyone in my life, just some family that I don't really talk to. Now that I can't hear jack shit, I really have absolutely no idea what I plan to do with my life. But like my dad likes to constantly remind me, I better figure it the fuck out pretty fast.

Deciding to go for a walk, I explore the place. Lexi catches me and starts scribbling something down on a piece of paper.

The gardens outside are really beautiful. If you want to go for a walk, they're outside the front door and to the left.

I follow her directions but never make it that far. Instead, I stop in my tracks when I see the woman lying in the grass staring at Oakside with a sketch pad in her lap.

She's way too young for me, but my gut says even though I don't know what my future holds, somehow I know that she's part of it.

CHAPTER 2

CARLEE

I am absolutely loving it here at Oakside. The grounds are beautiful and perfect for painting. It means so much to me that I get to paint here and what I do also helps all these wounded soldiers. This place looks like it should be on the cover of some home magazine or postcard—it's just so visually stunning.

I'm completely lost in the sketch I'm working on. The next painting that I'm planning on doing is of the old plantation home that has now been turned into Oakside. The tall two-story columns and the second floor two story balconies have me transfixed. So, I don't notice right away that a man is walking towards me until he sits beside me.

He has dark hair, a short beard, visible tattoos covering his arms and a tablet in his hand. I expect him to start talking to me, but instead, he types on the tablet. Maybe he came out here for some silence, but didn't want to be completely alone. If that's what he needs, I'm happy to sit here with him and keep him company.

But after a minute, he shows the tablet to me. The notepad is open with a question on it.

I'm Zane. What's your name?

I smile at him. "I'm Carlee. Are you one of the patients here?" I ask.

Instead of answering, he types on the tablet, turning it back towards me.

I've lost my hearing, so the tablet is how I communicate for now.

Nodding in understanding, I take the tablet from him.

Typing out what I want to say, I then hand it back to him. *I'm Carlee. It's nice to meet you.*

He smiles and moves his mouth almost like he's saying my name without any sound to it. When a tingle runs down my spine, I'm shocked. Before I can catch my breath, he starts typing again.

What are you doing here at Oakside?

I take it from him and type out my answer.

I'm doing some paintings to be displayed around Oakside both in the general areas and in the patient rooms. It's a great way for me to build up my portfolio. In addition, Noah asked me to teach a part-time art therapy class, so now, I will be here more often.

Ever since Noah and Lexi told us of Oakside, it's captured my imagination and I knew it would be important to me. When I told him I wanted to find a way to help the men and women here who are recovering, Noah suggested art therapy on a trial basis to see if it's something to add to their services here.

Handing the tablet back to him, I watch him read what I wrote. It's more than I'd normally share, but something compels me to be open with him. He smiles and types something on the tablet before he nods to my sketchbook in my lap and hands the tablet back to me.

Can I see what you're drawing?

I used to be pretty shy and closed off about my work, but my college professors were very good at pulling me out of my shell. With their guidance and encouragement, I'm open, but maybe a tiny bit reserved to share my sketches and my art.

"After all, why make art if no one sees it," one professor said. His words still stick with me.

Because art is very subjective, sharing can be either exciting or hor-rifying. Two people can look at the same piece and one can love it and the other hate it. But something tells me that this man isn't going to tear me down if he doesn't like what he sees. So, handing over my Sketchbook, I watch him look through it.

On the pages I've sketched the front of the Oakside main house building from a different perspective a few different times. I wanted to get the view from all sides. I've also sketched some of the other places on the property, like the barn and the garden. Also, there's one with the view down the oak-covered driveway heading onto the property.

Once he's done flipping through the book, he types on the tablet again before handing it to me.

These drawings are absolutely gorgeous. Can you take them and then turn them into your paintings?

I smile happily. The fact that he likes my work impacts me more than when friends, family, my professor, or any random stranger says how good they are and how much they enjoy them.

Though I feel like if he didn't, it would have completely devastated me.

Typing on the tablet, I answer his question.

Yeah, along with photos that I took as well. I could set up an easel out here, but I don't want to be in the way.

He takes the tablet back and types another message.

Can I ask how old you are?

Grinning big, I lock eyes with him. His expression is one of amusement mixed with something that I'm unfamiliar with. Even though it's a personal question, I'm trying not to read too much into it.

I like this man, but I doubt he's thinking about a relationship. He's probably just trying to be nice.

I'm twenty-two. I will be twenty-three at the end of the year. Now the same question for you.

I hand the tablet back to him and watch him type, a slight frown on his face. Does he not want to answer my question? But he types and then hands me the tablet again.

I'm thirty-five. Do you live around here, or are you just visiting?

Answering him, I type: *I grew up here and I just moved back after college. What about you? Where's home? Tell me more about you.* The urge to know more about him is irresistible. I've never felt this comfortable around someone that I just met. But I want to know more, lots more. It's kind of crazy that I want to know everything about him.

As I watch him, he types way longer than before. He is only using one hand because the other is wrapped up. Other than that, I don't see any visible injuries.

Then he hands the tablet back to me.

I grew up in North Carolina, and then I joined the Navy and became a SEAL. I love it. But now, I know they will medically discharge me. So I'm not sure what is in store for me. What else do you want to know?

I think for a moment. Hmm, what can I ask that isn't too personal?

So, all your family is back in North Carolina? Do you plan to move back there?

He types for a long time, even longer than before, and seems frustrated that he can only use one hand.

My parents are. But we aren't on good terms, so there is no reason for me to go back there. While I'm here, I guess that is part of what I have to figure out. I like the area, so I might stick around. Who knows? What about you? You plan to stay in the area?

It seems like I've been getting that question a lot lately. Now that I'm out of college, I guess people are expecting me to have a plan. But that doesn't mean that I do.

I think I'd like to stay here, but I guess it all depends on where I can get a job. Right now, I am only part-time here at Oakside. Though it would be a dream job to work here with everyone. I love it here. But I don't know if that is possible. So, I'm enjoying it while I can.

He types back. *I get that. It's a pivotal time in your life, but any choice you make will define the rest of your life, so don't rush into anything.*

Sounds like advice from someone who learned that lesson the hard way. I type back.

This time, he looks at me and then at Oakside, like he is lost in thought, before shaking his head and typing again.

I don't regret the choices I made more than the ones I didn't make.

Typing, I say, *My mom said that to me and my sister a lot growing up. We would regret the risks we didn't take more than the ones we did.*

That's good advice. You should listen to her. He types.

That is about the only good advice she ever had. Especially now, she just wants to push things on me that she wants. I start to delete it, but he stops me, reads it, and types back.

Like what?

Oh, it's nothing. We just met. I don't need to burden you with this.

Why did I bring this up? To a complete stranger, nonetheless. Maybe because I need someone to talk to, and not even my sister, who is one of my best friends, knows because I know she'd force me to tell Mom, and I'm just not ready.

He hands me back the tablet. *You are not a burden and you need to talk. I want to listen. It's not like I have much more to do anyway.*

Taking a deep breath, I admit the thing I've been trying to ignore for months now.

Well. My mom is pushing me to have kids. I think she is getting desperate and even suggesting IVF with a sperm donor now.

Biting my lip anxiously, I'm sure he is going to make up some excuse for needing to get back inside.

You don't want to have kids? he asks.

Yes, I want kids. But I just can't have them. I haven't told my mother yet. My ex broke up with me because I couldn't have kids, and she seemed extra desperate since the breakup to make it happen. My sister was married with a one-year-old when she was my age.

Doctors make mistakes all the time. Don't give up so soon if that's what you want, he says.

I shake my head, trying not to tear up. Ever since I was a kid, all I wanted was to be a mother. To have that taken from me was devastating. Even worse was I had no one around me at the time because my ex didn't call anyone. I was unconscious in the hospital, and my family was unaware. Waking up alone hurts and I'm still processing it all.

I was in a car accident. Long story short, they did emergency surgery, and my uterus was removed. My ex didn't call my family, so they still have no idea. They only knew I was in a car crash. I thought I needed to process it before I told my mom, but once I was healed, the harping from her got so much worse. But let's change the subject.

This is a lot to put on someone I just met.

His look once he reads what I wrote isn't one of pity but of understanding. We talk some more about light-hearted stuff like my work, things I've painted in the past, and what I studied in school. Before I know it, an *hour had passed.*

I hate to leave but I have a doctor's appointment. Will you be here tomorrow? I'd like to see you again, he says.

I'll be here. Maybe in the back this time. Come find me.   I tell him because I can't make it easy on him, right?

I will see you then. He types it with a smile on his handsome face.

Then as he enters the building, I watch him. My eyes take in his strong muscular body and the way he carries himself. I'm kind of surprised by the shiver that runs through my body.

When he pauses at the front door and looks back at me, it's as if he hates having to leave me here. Once the door closes behind him, it's like a connection has been severed. How in such a short time, can I feel the loss of his being near me? I have to say I don't like it, and I find it somewhat alarming.

It's a loss of something I didn't know I was missing. But now that I know it's out there, I don't want to be without it anymore.

CHAPTER 3

ZANE

I get to my room and start pacing the long room. It's comfortable and much better than any hospital room I've been in. There are hardwood floors, a comfortable bed, a desk, a living room with a couch, chairs, and a TV. It's nice that I have a private bathroom, too. The decorations are in keeping with the rustic feel the place has. I'd take Oakside over a hospital any day.

My room is on the second floor and looks out over the back of the property, so I get great views from here. But I can't see if Carlee is still on the front lawn or not. Now that my appointment is over, I would love to join her again on the lawn. But I don't want to scare her off either.

I have this draw to be around her even more. To be near her. But I don't want to scare her or put off stalker vibes. I'm sure the last thing she wants is an older, creepy man hanging around. Fuck, is she really only twenty-two? She is way too young, and I should stay away, but I know I won't be able to. I need to be near her, and I don't want to examine why this is.

Despite my injuries and lack of hearing, I feel like I am myself around her. The undeniable fact that I was fighting my cock from becoming hard the entire time I was with her tells the story. My body wants her, but my brain says she is too young, too pure for me and for my darkness to touch her.

The lights in my room flash, which is like a knock on the door to someone like me who can't hear anything. When I turn toward the door, Noah is standing there. He's one of us. When he was wounded in action, there was no place like Oakside that existed for him, so his wife started one. Now, we all get to benefit from it.

Noah wears scars on his face, neck, and arms. Many who are here have visible scars. Other than my hand, there won't be scars on me for people to see. They won't know until they realize I can't hear them.

I nod my head toward the couch, inviting him in. Noah is very hands-on with the patients. I guess having once been in our shoes helps him deal with those of us who end up here.

He walks over, sits, and picks up the tablet that's sitting on the coffee table.

How was the garden? he asks.

Of course, his wife told him I would be checking them out. I wouldn't expect anything less, but good communication between them.

I actually didn't make it that far. I met Carlee, and we got to talking. I'm not holding anything back and am going to be truthful.

I saw you, but I didn't know if you made it to the garden. She's really nice and incredibly talented. He watches me as I read what he wrote.

Yeah, she showed me her sketchbook. I can't wait to see what she paints.

Noah smiles, looking at me for a moment before he replies.

I could tell by the way you looked at her that there was something there. So, I signed you up for art therapy in her class.

My gut reaction was to say no, I'm not going. But I stopped myself. I guess one of the things that came out of not being able to react instantly is that I allow myself more time to think. Not only do I want to see what she does, but I want to see her paint, too. It can't hurt to get to spend more time with her.

Also, going to art therapy will show that I am trying and open to assisting in making sure that I can get out of here as soon as possible. Though I still have no idea what I'm going to do in civilian life. My top priority is to heal, and learn how to live my new life. If art therapy helps, then so be it.

But I'm going to need to address the other part of his statement.

She's way too young for me. I don't know what else to say, so I just leave it at that.

Says who? he asks.

Fuck, I don't know society? She's thirteen years younger than me, just out of college and starting her life. Here I am about to be medically retired from the military, having lost my hearing. I have no idea what I'm going to do with the rest of my life or how I'm going to support myself, much less someone else.

I could go on and on about how she doesn't need to be involved in all of that. How no dating probably isn't even on the table because anyone that I end up with would just end up taking care of me. How is that fair to them?

Noah types back. *Time and time again, I pushed Lexi away. I knew it was the right thing to do, yet I couldn't help pulling her to me over and over because I couldn't stand the thought of not having her in my life. I thought that if she was saddled with me, she'd spend her life taking care of me. That's when I was at my darkest point and couldn't see the light through the trees.*

What changed? I ask.

A beautiful blonde barged her way into my life. I finally realized that sometimes life throws you a curveball, and you watch your dreams crash and burn around you, but then you have to find new dreams. She looked me straight in the eye and told me that I will fight and that I would be okay and that I did not have another choice. When I needed her the most, she charged into my life. Once I began my recovery, I came to the other side. I couldn't imagine my life without her. I fight every day to make sure that I'm the one taking care of her.

He has a huge smile on his face, and I can tell without a shadow of a doubt how much he is in love with her. I can only imagine the battle he had with all the severe burns and injuries that he had. The healing he had to go through must have been hard and intense.

He made it out on the other side, and he's living his life. His dreams may have changed, but it's clear he's living the life he was meant to. He's right where he needs to be.

I've never been an overly patient man, but apparently that's what I'm going to need to be right now. Maybe giving it time and letting the dust settle will help me find my future.

Grinning, I tell him honestly, *You got lucky with Lexi. I guess at this point, only time will tell, and I'm not in a position to rush anything. But I do want to get to know Carlee better. And then, under any other circumstances, I'd be upset that you signed me up for art therapy, but in this case, thank you.*

We say our goodbyes, and he leaves, but I sit there thinking and going over everything that he just said.

If the boys in my unit ever found out that I was doing art therapy, I would never hear the end of it. But all the ribbing in the world could not keep me away from Carlee.

CHAPTER 4

CARLEE

My sister, Kaylee, and I have always been really close. I love that even now that she is married with a kid, I am able to head to her house for dinner when I don't want to cook. A few times a week after work, she will invite me to stop by, have dinner, and then load me up with leftovers to take home so that I'm able to warm something up when I am not eating with them.

Since I've been home from college, it's become our routine. I absolutely love it. And spending time with my niece and brother-in-law is always a plus. Because, let's be honest, they are some of my favorite people.

When I step up on my sister's front porch and knock on the door, I'm excited when I can smell her meatloaf. My brother-in-law, Brian answers the door and rolls his eyes when he sees me. He has on his reading glasses, indicates to me he was probably answering some last-minute work emails.

"How many times do we have to tell you that you are family and you do not need to knock? You come over here enough to have family privileges." Even though he says it in a playful way, his tone is totally serious.

"No thanks. I'll knock because just the thought of walking in on something I shouldn't is enough to traumatize me forever." I give him a hug and walk past him into the kitchen, where I know I'll find my sister.

I've read multiple books where one person walks into the house without knocking, and the couple is having fun time, and they see something they wish they hadn't. I'm not going to be one of those people, especially with my sister. So even though my logical brain says she's cooking dinner, and my niece is home, I'm still just not going to risk it.

"Is Brian still trying to convince you that you don't have to knock when you get here?" my sister asks, stopping what she's doing and giving me a hug when I walk into the kitchen.

"He's trying, but it's never going to happen. You read the books, I do, so you understand," I say.

Brian laughs as he comes into the kitchen, shaking his head.

"Where is Liz?" I ask about my niece because I really want to talk to my sister, but this is not the kind of talk my six-year-old niece needs to be involved in.

"She's in her room doing her homework. Is everything okay?" my sister asks as I sit down on the kitchen island.

"Well, I met one of the Oakside patients today. He and I sat and talked for a little while. I had never met him before, but there was just this connection that I can't describe."

Her face lights up. "That is exactly how I felt when I met Brian. There was just this unmistakable connection, and it felt like I had been missing it in my life the whole time. I woke up that morning not knowing I was missing it, and then, by that evening, it felt like the other half of my soul had been found. So, tell me all about him." Her smile is growing even larger than I thought possible.

"Well, he's a Navy SEAL, but he thinks that he's going to be medically discharged because he lost his hearing. We were communicating via the tablet that they had given him. Though he is thirty-five, so there's a little age gap there. We sat and talked for over an hour. Then he asked about my paintings and looked at my sketchbook..."

"Wait, wait, wait! You let him look at your sketchbook?"

"Yeah, he asked, and all I heard was my professor's voice in the back of my head saying how I need to be more open with my art," I say.

"But I've been asking for years, and you still won't let me look at it," she says, giving me puppy-dog eyes.

"Because you're my sister. It's different. I have to look at you every day, and if you hated it, then I don't know how that would affect our relationship."

"I love your paintings. Why would I hate the stuff in your sketches?"

"Because there is a difference. But you're getting off-topic here. He's thirty-five and a patient at Oakside. I feel like there are so many things indicating that this can't happen."

I'm trying to get back to the point, yet I'm distracted by her at the same time.

"Who says it can't happen? The age gap is nothing especially because age is just a number. You can learn ASL, as I'm sure he will be. Then you'll be able to communicate with him." She turns back to dinner, acting like it's nothing that I just told her about possibly meeting the man of my dreams.

"You should do it, Aunt Carlee. It's really easy. I learned ASL because one of the girls in my after-school group is deaf, and I wanted to be her friend. Now we talk all the time, and it's like our secret language. The teacher even asks me to translate because I'm better than she is at it." My niece informs me as she comes bouncing down the stairs.

"Mom, is dinner ready? I'm starving."

"Yep, why don't you help me set the table?" My sister says, giving me a look, telling me that this conversation is not over just because my niece walked into the room. I know that as soon as dinner is over, she's going to pull me away and continue to interrogate me.

All throughout dinner, I'm thinking about what my sister said. None of the objections I had are really a reason that we can't be together. That's when I realize it was my mother's voice in my head. She's going to think he's too old and not the right one to have children with and get married. But since I can't have kids, that shouldn't even be a consideration.

The problem is, I haven't told anyone, making it hard to talk this out with my sister or any of my family. I really need to make a friend and spill it all out and get an outside opinion on all of this. Though I did not leave college with many close friends because I wanted to keep my head down and stay out of the drama.

I can't ignore that there's something urging me I need to open up about this to my sister. The real reason that I haven't told her yet is I'm worried she's going to tell our mom. But surely she won't do that until I'm ready.

After dinner, just as I thought, she leaves Brian and Liz to do the dishes. Then she pulls me to her bedroom at the back of the house, closes the door, and flops down on her bed.

"Okay, tell me more. There's something I can tell you're not telling me," she says.

The guilt hits me, so I feel like the time is right to talk to her. "Okay, I'm going to tell you something, but please don't be mad. Just know that I've been processing and dealing with this. You have to promise before you even know what I'm going to tell you that you won't say anything to Mom. Right now, I'm not ready to have this conversation with her."

My sister sits up instantly, her smile gone and her face serious as she stares at me.

"I swear. But now you're scaring me. Is everything okay?"

Walking over to her, I sit down next to her. I don't think I can look her in the eye when I say this.

"Remember the car accident that I was in? The one where you guys didn't know about until I was leaving the hospital?"

"Yeah, I think the best thing you ever did was dump that guy," my sister says.

To say she was ready to kill my ex for not calling them is an understatement.

"The accident was more serious than I let on to you all. While I was in emergency surgery, I'm not sure what exactly happened, but a part of the tree was lodged in me. To save my life, they had to remove my uterus, which means I can no longer have children. The dumbass broke up with me because I would not be able to give him kids." I cringe, waiting for my sister's reaction.

I don't know what I expected. Yelling, screeching, several 'oh my gods' maybe. Instead, her arms wrap around me, and she holds me tight. I don't know if this hug is because she thinks I need it or because she needs it, so I wrap my arms around her, and we don't move.

This is how her husband finds us several minutes later when he comes in asking if we want dessert.

"We're going to need a pint of chocolate ice cream," my sister says, and you can hear the tears and emotion in her voice.

She looks at her husband over my shoulder, and they seem to have one of those silent married couple conversations. He doesn't ask any questions as he heads back to the kitchen, I'm sure, to get ice cream spoons.

"I am so sorry that you are dealing with this, and I understand that you had to have to have time to process. I'm not upset that you haven't told me before now, but I wish I had been there at the hospital for you. And I promise I won't tell Mom. Though, you know it would get her off your back about having kids."

"Mom thinks all I'm good for is having children. What the heck is she going to think if I can't have them? She going to start forcing me to be a foster parent so I can adopt, or I don't even want to know what she'll come up with. Eventually, I know I'll have to deal with her whole 'You need have kids' speech. For now, I just need it to be like this because I don't think I've fully processed all of it yet. And since I've just met Zane, I don't even know what to think, but less to say. This is a big reason why I have not dated."

"Well, make sure that you're honest and open with him. That's all you can do when you're dating is to be honest and open. The right guy won't care."

"I told him I couldn't have kids and a little about the accident. Which is really weird because he was the first person that I've told, and he was a complete stranger. It was so out of character for me. But he still wants to see me again tomorrow, so I didn't send him running. I'm guessing that's a good sign."

"That's the best sign. I know you've always wanted to be a mom, but adoption is always on the table. Just make sure that you do it for yourself and not because Mom's pushing you or because you feel like you have to keep a guy in your life."

It's right then that Brian walks in with the ice cream, two spoons, a box of tissues, and some chocolate candy.

"I'll put Liz to bed tonight. You two have it out, and you know you're welcome to crash on the couch if you need to," he says to me.

"Why can't you have a brother for me?" I ask, only half joking.

"Because I was destined to be an only child," he laughs, as he leaves the room.

"So romantic comedy?" my sister asked, referring to the movie we're going to watch.

This is our thing. We get situated in the bed, crack open the ice cream, and put on some cheesy romantic comedy movie that we've seen a million times and don't have to pay attention to as we randomly talk and eat.

I didn't realize how badly I needed this and how soothing to my soul it is.

CHAPTER 5

ZANE

Today is my first art therapy class. Over the last few days, I've been getting to know Carlee. Every time I see her sitting out in the sun sketching in her sketchbook, I can't ignore her. Whether it's her beauty, or her serenity or something indefinable, I'm drawn to her and like spending time with her. Without a doubt in my mind, I am convinced that she's meant to be in my life. I just know.

Even though I'm falling harder for her than I have any right to, there's no way in hell I can walk away, either. Since dawn, I've been waiting for the therapy class to begin. Not because I think the therapy is going to help me, but because I get to see Carlee. I get to see her doing what she loves. I'm hoping I can convince her to spend some time with me after class too.

I'm watching more of the sign language videos that Faith is assigning to me. All my free time is dedicated to learning it. I'm guessing most of the staff around here knows it, because they learned when Faith's husband was here. Carlee has even been learning it, so I am looking forward to being able to talk more with her without the tablet's hindrance.

I'm so zoned in the videos that I jump when the lights flicker indicating someone is at the door

When I look up, I find Noah standing there with a concerned look on his face.

Turning off the videos, I wave him to sit down while I open the notepad on my tablet.

Are you okay? You seem really out of sorts today, Noah says.

Yeah, to be honest, I'm a bit nervous about this art therapy. I figured I would go over some of my videos to distract myself, I tell him truthfully.

I *think you will really benefit from art therapy. It teaches you to look at things a different way while letting go and just being. Plus, I think the teacher is pretty good if I do say so myself,* he smirks.

At the mention of Carlee, I break into a smile. There's no hiding it that I've got it bad, but I wouldn't have it any other way.

The teacher definitely has something to do with me being nervous about this class. This is what she does and what she loves, and I can't wait to experience it. Though art is not really my thing. I think the fanciest I've gotten with drawing is stick figures with clothes on them, I admit.

Noah nods. *Yeah, most of the guys who join the military have no artistic experience. It's all about giving you another way to think through things and to see things from another point of view. You will do great. I'll talk with you again with you after the class.*

Once Noah leaves, I finish the video I was watching, and then head down to the dining room. Since the class is right after lunch, I'm going to eat now. As I watch all the people around me, I try to remember what the sounds of being in a dining hall were like.

The dishes clattering, people talking, and silverware hitting the plates as people ate. Even the sound of laughter, I still remember and can hear it in my dreams. Though most of my dreams have been completely full of Carlee.

Going early to the art class, I find I'm the first one there and Carlee is still setting up. I tap my knuckles on the door frame to get her attention. She looks up, smiling and waves before walking right over to me and takes the tablet. Over the past few days, it's become our little tradition. *Even though Noah signed me up for your class, I'm really eager to be here. I want to see what you do and what you get excited about. Don't expect too much from me. Stick figures are about the top of my ability.*

That causes her to laugh as she reads it. At this moment, I would give anything to hear that laugh.

She continues to type away on the tablet before handing it back to me.

I assume most soldiers don't join the military because they have a fantastic art ability, so we're starting super easy today, I promise. And I'll give instructions to the class and then I'll come back and type it out for you.

Thank you. Hopefully, one day soon, just having an interpreter will be enough. I'm pushing hard to learn. As it'll give me back more freedom.

I've been learning it, too. My niece has been super excited about teaching me. Though I think what she's most excited about is being able to have a conversation that her parents don't understand. It's gotten her in trouble at the dining room table a few times already.

I laugh at that one, but then she looks at me weirdly, so I take the tablet back and ask her if everything is okay. She smiles and types, handing it back to me.

Everything is great. That was just the first time I got to hear you laugh. I guess for some reason, I didn't think that you would still be able to laugh, which means you could probably still talk if you needed to. But I think sign language is the best option for you. It'll be like we have our own secret code and private language when we talk around other people. She smiles mischievously as others start to files into the room.

Taking a seat near the front of the room because I want to get the best view of her as other people start taking their seats. She greets each person with a smile, though not quite as big as the one with which she greeted me.

My ASL teacher showed me this really neat feature on the tablet that I can turn on and it will dictate what's being said around me. So as Carlee starts talking, I turn it on. She is moving around as she speaks, so it's not perfect, but I can get a sense of what she's saying.

After a few minutes, everyone picks up their paintbrushes and start painting. When she walks over to me, I exit out of the program and open up the notepad. She picks up the tablet, types out the instructions for me.

Once I start, she heads back to the front of the room and begins painting on a canvas. I am mesmerized watching her go at it. Painting a flower from nothing but the image in her mind is something I want to try. When I attempt to replicate what she does, by the time I'm done, it looks like a five-year-old tried to copy a masterpiece.

She walks around looking at everyone's paintings, giving tips and advice. I can tell she loves it because she has a beaming smile on her face the entire time. When she gets to me, she places her hand on my arm before she picks up the tablet.

I love her soft skin on mine. The feeling is a shock to my system and has my cock taking notice. I'm always fighting getting hard with her around, but when she has her hands on me it's impossible to hide.

That is much better than a stick figure. She types, handing the tablet back to me.

Well, I had a really good teacher, and I just tried to mimic what she did. I offer her a small smile. Yeah, I used to be so much better at flirting.

With fascination, I watch a light blush coat her cheeks as she types out on the tablet again. Fuck, she is so sexy, and she doesn't even know it.

It just takes practice. You'll get the hang of it in no time.

With you as my teacher, I have no doubt. Will you join me for a walk in the garden after class? I ask.

Normally, I wouldn't ask something like that in the middle of class surrounded by everyone, but being that we are using the tablet, no one else can hear the conversation. So I feel comfortable asking her.

Yes, I'd like that. I have to clean up afterward, but once I'm done, I can go.

I'll stay and help you clean up. I offer my help. Every extra minute with Carlee is a bonus.

Nodding, her eyes light up and she smiles. Then she hands me back the tablet and moves on to helping the next person.

Taking another look at my painting, I'm dubious and am wondering what I should get out of this class. If it's hope that I'll find a new skill, well, this definitely, isn't it. I've seen kids draw better pictures in elementary school than in my effort at painting. Still, I'm pretty proud of it. But it's better than anything I have drawn or painted before. When I look back at Carlee's painting at the front of the class, I notice she put her signature in the bottom right-hand corner. So, I do the same with my signature. I think that means my painting is done.

Thankfully, Carlee walks back up to the front of the class, and I turn the transcribe app back on right before she starts talking. Wrapping up the class, she tells everyone to leave their paintings to dry and to pick them up next week.

As everyone leaves, I help Carlee clean the brushes, put the paint away, and move them to the side of the room so they can dry well. She puts the easels away and does some other cleaning.

Once the room is tidy, she smiles at me and nods towards the door. I follow her outside to the garden that I haven't been to yet. Spending time with her the last couple of days on the lawn has been my priority. This is the first time I get to see the garden, and it really is beautiful.

Stone walls line the garden, and there are plenty of different seating areas, including a swing. There's a creek with a little waterfall that runs through it, walking paths with flowers and garden decorations. It's peaceful, colorful and charming.

Carlee leads us to the swing, where she sits and reaches for my tablet.

I plan on painting the garden next. I think, so far, it's probably my favorite place on the whole property, she says.

I can see why. It's absolutely beautiful and serene. I tell her.

We sit and talk and I tell her about Faith coming in and working with me on my ASL lessons. It's fun to show her a few of the signs that I've learned.

She surprises me by telling me she is also taking some lessons, so she'll be able to talk to me. After telling me how her paintings are going, she drops the biggest bombshell.

I told my sister about the accident and how I couldn't have kids.

I take a moment to think about my response to Carlee telling her, but I can't get a read on how it went either.

How did it go? I ask hesitantly.

Pretty well. She promised not to tell my mom just yet. But agrees that I should tell her. Though she also understands my reasoning for not telling her right now. We cried together. She felt really guilty about not being there when the accident happened, but she couldn't have been because she didn't know. By the time I was able to call them and tell them I was being released from the hospital, I was numb.

After we finished crying, we ate our weight in ice cream, watched a movie and had a sister night that we really needed.

As I'm reading this, it makes me glad her sister is supporting her. It was a big deal for her to talk to her sister and get it out into the open.

As we swing, she rests her head on my shoulder and I can tell that she doesn't need my words, just me being here for her right now. So we sit and swing and watch the world around us.

Supporting her like this is easy. I've got this.

CHAPTER 6

CARLEE

It's been a few weeks of getting to know Zane and him being in my art therapy class. We've both been learning ASL, so we've been able to have some shorter conversations without using the tablet.

On my days off, I'm finding little excuses to be at Oakside so that I can spend some time with him. Every day, he asks if I'll be back tomorrow and tries to make plans to spend some time with me.

Today, he has asked me to meet him in his room. It will be the first time I get to see where he's been staying. I'm walking down the hallway, and I stop just before I reach his door. Normally, I'd knock, but he's not going to hear it. Walking into his room uninvited doesn't seem right either. Thankfully, there's a nurse in the hallway, and she walks over and smiles at me.

"My name is Kaitlyn, and I'm a nurse here. Can I help you with something?" she asks.

"I'm here to see Zane, but I'm not sure how to knock on his door. Since he won't be able to hear it, how will he know I'm here?" I ask, feeling silly about not knowing and about the way I worded it.

"Oh, this switch right here. It's kind of like a doorbell, but will flash the lights, letting him know that someone's there," she says, pointing to a button next to his door that does look like a doorbell. I thought it was just a light switch.

I press the button, and a minute later, Zane opens the door. He's dressed in jeans and a button-down shirt with the sleeves rolled up showing off his gorgeous tattoos. A huge smile lights up his face and his sea-blue eyes light up. He holds up a finger, indicating that I should wait a moment as he goes into the room to grab something, and when he comes back out with his tablet.

Then he steps into the hallway, closes the door behind him, and nods to Kaitlyn. Together we walk to the lobby and out the front door.

As we step off the front porch, he pauses for a minute as the sun hits the sharp planes of his face. I take a moment to enjoy his masculine beauty and drink in this time with him. After a moment, he takes my hand in his, and leads me to the garden.

The feel of his big hand holding mine makes my heart race. My hand fits in his perfectly, and just this simple act makes me feel so safe. It does funny things to me, but I try to play it off cool, so maybe he will do it again some other time.

He leads me towards the little waterfall at the back of the garden, where there is a little picnic all set up. When I stop, I see his eyes are on me.

Is this for us? I sign.

He nods with a smile, leading me over to where the blanket is already set up. We sit, and he pulls out sandwiches, fruit, chips, and my favorite, Oreo cookies.

Then he pulls out the tablet and starts typing.

I love being out here in the garden, so I figured we could have a picnic lunch today instead of sitting on the lawn.

It's perfect. I smile at him as we begin eating lunch.

Will you tell me more about your family? he asks.

Thank goodness for the speech to text feature on the tablet.

My mom was always the traditional stay-at-home mom who, as soon as we were old enough, insisted my sister and I have kids so that she could be a grandmother. She's never worked a day in her life outside the home. She went straight from her parent's house to college to live with my dad. So, she doesn't understand why I want my own job and to stand on my own two feet. My dad is slow and steady, a hard worker, and the first to fix things on his own before bringing anyone else in for help. He taught me lots of skills and also encouraged my painting.

What about your sister? he asks.

She is my best friend. It wasn't always like that growing up. We fought a lot. Her husband Brian is so good to her and doesn't care how much I crash dinner at their house. And my niece, Liz, is probably the coolest six-year-old I've ever met.

We pause for a minute and then I look back up at him and take the tablet before he gets a chance to write anything else.

My sister has been checking on me since I told her about not being able to have kids. When my mom she tried to harp on me about why I don't try to reconnect with Eric, she stopped her.

Is he the ex who dumped you because you can't have kids?

Yeah, and after how he handled the car crash, I'd have ended things with him anyway. Who doesn't call someone's family when they have to have emergency surgery?

After all the heavy talk, I try to lighten things up, but apparently, I just make it awkward.

If I didn't know any better, I'd say this kind of feels like a date. I joke with him.

He looks at me for a moment like he's not quite sure what to say.

What if it is?

I'm so caught off guard by the question that I just sit there staring at it, reading it over and over again. But then I decide to tell him the truth.

It would be the best date I've been on in five years. I tell him honestly.

Come on, this is all I can do. Lunch in a garden here at Oakside? You had to have been on better dates. Even an actual restaurant would be better than this.

I've had a couple of dates at restaurants, but the problem is I'm very open about not being able to have kids. I'm upfront about it because I don't want to get involved with someone and then it becomes an issue. Those guys that want children I have found will end the date really early. Though, I can't blame them. But then the ones who are okay with it and don't want kids at all, I'm not interested in them either. Because I still want to find a way to be a mother.

I watch him read it, ready for him to run, because I know he said he had no plans of having kids and I desperately want to be a mom.

The right one won't run away because you want to be a mother. The right one will want a family with you, he says.

But I notice that he didn't mention what he wants.

Yeah, that's what I figure, too, but it makes dating really hard, hence why I'm still a virgin, at almost twenty-three.

I don't know what gave me the courage to tell him that, but something's telling me to be totally honest, put all my issues up front, and if he stays, then so be it. But I doubt he's going to. Older men like him want experienced women.

He's drinking some of his water as he's reading what I wrote, and I can tell the moment he reads about me being a virgin because he actually chokes on his drink.

When he looks over at me, his eyes are soft, but I can tell he's definitely looking at me differently now, and I absolutely hate it. So, I take the tablet back from him set on changing the subject.

Have you been out to the barn and done any of the horseback riding that they have here? I ask.

He allows the conversation change, but there's definitely a shift in the mood.

I have to wait until I get the okay from my doctor and my hand heals, but after that I plan to.

Since I notice he doesn't invite me to join him, he must be looking for a way to end this gracefully.

As I quickly finish my lunch, we talk about the art therapy classes and then I make an excuse about needing to go talk to Noah and Lexi.

Time with Zane was good while it lasted. I just wish for once I'd find the guy that's going to stick around because getting my hopes up, only to have them crushed is heartbreaking. It doesn't help that I'm starting to have feelings for him.

CHAPTER 7

CarleeWhen I admitted to Zane that I was a virgin, it definitely changed things between us. I thought for sure he was going to run for the hills, and that would be the end of our spending time together. Especially after the way the date ended.

But the next day, he found me out on the back lawn sketching a few of the guys playing football. Then the following day, he found me over in the barn sketching some of the horses, and today, he found me in the garden.

Only today he doesn't have the tablet with him. We're both communicating with ASL. Thank goodness those lessons are paying off.

Can I ask you a question? he asks.

My body tenses because I'm absolutely sure it's going to be about me being a virgin or any part of the conversation we had at our picnic. But I nod and wait to see what he wants to know.

Faith told me that I need to start using ASL more frequently. I was wondering if we could talk strictly in ASL? he signs.

I think that would be good practice for both of us. I agree.

It will definitely be an easier conversation than typing into a tablet and waiting for the other to read it and then passing the tablet back and forth.

Have you started any of the paintings? he asks.

Yeah, at home. I'm working on one of the driveways with the trees covering it.

I can't wait to see it.

It's the one Lexi requested. She wants to put in the lobby.

I bet that driveway is beautiful in fall when all the leaves start to change, he says.

It's then, as he is signing, that I notice his hand isn't bandaged up anymore. So, gently reaching out, I take his hand into mine. Without thinking anything of it, I want to get a look at how it is healing.

This is the first time we've touched each other since the picnic. It's hard to ignore the sparks I feel where his skin touches mine. Judging by the look in his eyes, he feels it too.

Pushing the dirty thoughts which are zinging through my mind of what his hands could be doing to me, I focus on examining it.

His hand is healing nicely. The stitches have been removed, and the scars are a red, almost purple color. They will lighten over time and eventually the scars will look like part of his hand.

Tracing my finger over the scars, I see they make an interesting pattern on his hand. He doesn't move, but lets me run my finger over them again and again. Feeling a shiver down my spine, I notice how big his hand is and calloused, and how it might feel all over my body. I remind myself that this is a man who used them in dangerous situations. When I look up at him, his eyes are on mine and the heat that's in them is unmistakable.

Sorry. Your hand looks like it's healing really well. I apologize, trying to defuse the situation.

He doesn't say anything. Instead, he just reaches out, takes my hand, turns it over, and runs his fingers over the lines on my palm like I did the scars on his hand. He traces the lines slowly, but his eyes are on my face. I feel the movement of his finger all the way down to my core. My nipples are hard, and I'm sure he can see them through my shirt and the thin bra that I'm wearing. My clit tingles and all I want to do is move to get some relief. Without even checking, I know I'm soaking wet and will need to change my panties.

This simple little gesture from him has turned me on, and I wonder if it did the same for him. When I look down at his hand holding mine, I chance a quick glance at his lap. His cock is hard behind his jeans, clear as day. How does this simple interaction have such a big effect on us both?

My eyes meet his again and we stare at each other for just a moment, neither of us saying anything. The intense emotion between us is too much, and I pull my hand away and open my sketchbook again.

He lies down in the grass beside me, something that he loves doing. While I sketch for the day, he enjoys soaking up the rays and simply being beside me.

Only today, instead of sketching the many beautiful locations around Oakside, I find myself drawing the same pattern over and over again. Looking down at my work, I see that I've sketched the pattern of scars on his hand.

When he looks over at me again, I decide to ask what is on my mind.

Why do you like being out in the sun so much?

He doesn't answer right away, but just soaks in the sun for another minute.

I've been on a lot of missions. I can't talk about the details. But many of them were spent sitting inside for hours waiting for a split-second opportunity. Then after my accident, I was in the hospital for so long I missed being outside. Now, I don't take it for granted anymore.

I know he is letting me know not to ask questions about his missions. And I get the message loud and clear. I don't want to make him uncomfortable and drag all that up anyway.

So, a weird question. If you can't talk about your missions but you have to talk about what happened over there as part of your treatment, how does that work?

I've talked with Lexi and Noah quite a bit, learning how this place works. The men and women, who are patients here, have to talk in therapy and be cleared by the therapists before they're able to be discharged. It's one of the requirements so they can make sure that the men and women here are starting out on the best possible foot, whether it's going back into service or starting a new life in the civilian world.

Dr. Tate has the clearance necessary for me to talk to him. The military has assigned therapists to many of us who were on classified assignments. When did you know you wanted to be an artist?

I recognize that he's trying to change the subject and I guess this is a topic that makes him uncomfortable. So, I flow with his question.

In elementary school, we had art class once a week, and it was always my favorite. I think I was in fifth grade when I realized that I wanted to learn more about art and textures and all that could make me a better artist. When I asked my parents if I could take some art classes, they actually agreed. I tried sculpting, but that wasn't my thing, and neither was pottery nor making anything 'useful.' I use air quotes around the words that my mom would say because apparently paintings that just hang on the wall aren't very useful around the house.

Who said your art isn't useful? He asks me, catching on.

My mother. The best way I can describe her is old-fashioned. Women having a career is something to be looked down upon. Even more so when that career is art.

Well, I already don't like your mother. I hope you know that's bullshit. You're following your passion and making money too. That's an amazing accomplishment and you should be proud of it.

His words touch me, and my eyes tear up. I don't want him to think I'm this emotional basket case. But outside of my sister's encouragement, no one else has really pushed me to do what I wanted or thought that I was doing a good job on this career path. So, it makes his words mean all that much more.

I need to be careful. This man is doing dangerous things to my heart.

CHAPTER 8

ZANE

I know I should stay away from Carlee, especially after the picnic, and she admitted that she was a virgin. The problem is that my dreams at night now consist of claiming her as my own. She deserves better, but I'll kill anyone else who tries to put a hand on her.

It makes no sense, and I haven't even tried to talk to anyone about how it makes me feel. I know the simple answer is to leave her alone. They will tell me to let her live her life, and my feelings will sort themselves out. But not being around her, isn't an option either.

So, while I try to figure myself out, I go look for her. It's our own little game of hide-and-seek. It's been a few days since the first time she saw the scars on my hand, but every time we sit down together, she'll take my hand and trace those scars again.

I was self-conscious about the scars. They stand out pretty easily against my skin, but the fact that Carlee loves tracing her hands over them and the way her body reacts when she does, I'm damn proud of those scars and happy they intrigue her.

It's foreplay. A kind I've never experienced before, and I'm enjoying the hell out of it. Nor do I think I will ever find it again. Fuck if I can stop it, anyway.

As I enter the lobby, getting ready to go outside and find her, Noah steps into my path. While I want to ignore him and go find Carlee, it's not an option. I don't want to talk and waste time here, but he's been nothing but nice and supportive, so I can't be an asshole to him.

She's doing some sketches of my place today. Take the path over by the parking area. He signs, pointing in that direction.

So, I head out to explore a new area that I have not yet been to. Off the parking lot, there's a beautiful walkway that is paved and cuts between the trees. It has inviting benches along the way. Coming out on the other side of the path is a beautiful Colonial home, and sitting on the front porch swing is my girl.

I like the sound of that, my girl. I want her to be mine, but I don't know if she really truly ever will be. But for now, for a time, she is mine.

As I make my way over to her, she looks up and sees me and there is a huge smile lighting up her face.

How did you find me? she asks.

Noah stopped me in the lobby and told me. I tell her as I approach the porch and stop at the steps.

That's cheating. She says, but pats the spot on the swing next to her. I climb up the brick porch steps and join her.

When I glance over at her sketchpad to see what she's drawing, all I see are a bunch of lines that look nothing like anything around us.

What is that? I ask her.

She looks at me hesitantly, but then reaches for my hand, and my dick instantly goes hard. Then she turns my hand over, runs a finger over the scars, and points to the sketch pad.

That's when I realize that the pattern on the sketch pad is the same pattern as my scars. I flip back through a few pages and realize that all she's been sketching lately is that same pattern over and over and over again.

I can tell that having me look at her sketchbook makes her nervous, but she doesn't stop me. When I look back up at her, she tries to change the subject.

Why did you decide to join the military?

There was really nothing for me back home. My dad and I had completely different opinions. Mom agreed with him just to keep the peace. Why she's still with him, I will never know. I think she's just scared that she won't be able to make it on her own. Even though I've offered to help her before, she never takes me up on it. So in short, I saw it as my ticket out of town because I knew college wasn't going to be for me. I answer honestly.

I knew I was going to go to college, but my mom thought it was just a waste of time, especially since I was going to get an art degree. She thought I should use that time looking for a husband. I can't prove it, but I'm pretty sure my dad convinced her that I'd have a good chance of finding someone in college. Needless to say, when I started dating Eric, she was ecstatic. She still asks me if I'm sure we can't work things out, and I can't tell her the truth without telling her I can no longer have kids, and I am just not ready for that yet.

A small irrational part of me is angry at her mother for suggesting that she be with any other guy but me. Her mother doesn't even know I exist, so I get how crazy it all sounds. Nevertheless, the thought of her with anyone else drives me mad.

So, you got out and went to college. What made you decide to come back?

My sister. I wanted to be near her, and I wanted to be here to see my niece grow up. She's the closest thing I'll have to a kid, so I want to be able to spoil her as much as I can and then send her back to my sister to deal with the consequences. She says it with a slightly evil smile.

Oh, you want to be the fun aunt. I think it would be fun to be the fun uncle. I say with a chuckle.

I can see Carlee and me taking her niece out for ice cream and a day at the beach. Then bringing her home tired with a huge smile on her face. Once we've dropped her off at her parents, we'd go home to spend the rest of the night making love over and over again until she passed out.

Right away, I clear those thoughts because there's no way that they're going to happen. Eventually, I will get cleared from Oakside and discharged. I have to figure out what to do with the rest of my life. I doubt the sweet, young, beautiful girl is going to want to be tied to a damaged older man like me.

CHAPTER 9

CARLEE

"Is everything okay? You look like you're stuck in your own head today," Lexi asks as I walk back into the lobby after spending the afternoon with Zane on the lawn.

"Well, I guess that's because I am stuck in my head. Trying to figure some things out. I don't have a lot of close friends to call, so I might go visit my sister's and see what advice she has offer." I tell her, trying to shake out thoughts of Zane from my head.

"Listen, some of the girls who work here, we all do a girls' night at least once a month. Coincidentally, we're having one tonight. You should come. The guys go back, and they barbecue and chat and we girls take over my sunroom. This is an opportunity for you to get it all out and maybe get some good advice. There's great food, and drinks, if you need them. We're all willing to listen, troubleshoot, and give our opinions. Hopefully, we can help you out."

I almost said no and passed, but stopped myself. Though I don't know what the future holds for me, but while I'm here, it wouldn't hurt to have some friends. I love my sister to death, but I could use some other people to talk to as well. Maybe even find some friends to go out with and get me out of the house.

"You know, I think I will join you. What can I bring? Drinks? Dessert?"

We meet at 6 p.m. at my house next door. You don't have to bring anything, but if you want to bring a dessert, I know none of the ladies will turn it down." Lexi gives me a hug-before she is pulled away by someone in the lobby.Packing up my stuff, I go home to spend some time on the painting that I'm working on. I'm almost done with the view of the driveway, but I can't stop thinking about what Zane said, how beautiful it must look at fall as all the leaves start to change.

I hope I'll be around to see it happen. As much as I would love to put some space between me and my mother, I really want to be close to my sister and my niece. Also, I like this area, and there's the added bonus of how much I enjoy working with the people here at Oakside. When I'm done painting, I take a quick shower to wash off any paint that I have on me. After applying a little makeup, I go to the kitchen and make the brownies that my niece loves. Hopefully, that means these girls will love it too.

By the time I get to Lexi's house, I'm a few minutes early. While I'm sure that it's okay, I'm relieved to see there are several cars already in the driveway.

When I knock on the door, it's Faith, the ASL teacher at Oakside who answers the door.

"Come on in. Lexi said you'd be joining us today. She's just finishing up dinner." Faith leads me toward the kitchen at the back of the house.There are quite a few more people here than I expected. Paisley and her husband Easton, Jake and his fiancé Kassi, who recently got engaged.

The nurse Kaitlyn that I met the other day is here with a man who I assume is her husband because his arm is around her waist.

"I'm sure you recognize some people here, but this guy is my husband, Logan. He can hear you. He is not able to speak, so we use sign language to communicate. Over there is Gavin and his wife, Lauren. Even though he can hear, he won't be able to see the sign language, so in order to communicate with everyone, we generally talk at the same time we sign. This cute little thing over here is Noah's sister, Lucy. She's recently met someone, but is being super tight-lipped about it and not sharing a thing." At her words, Lucy's face lights up, and she giggles.

Faith continues, introducing me to everyone around the room.

"All right, let's get the show on the road, guys and kids. Food is here in the kitchen. Help yourself to anything that you want or need. The bathroom is under the stairs. No girls are allowed on the back porch, and no guys are allowed in the sunroom. If you need to talk to your spouse, you need to do it in the kitchen or a common room. Or wait until we're done."

A pang of jealousy hits me as everyone turns to their partners, giving hugs and kisses. Being one of the only single people here, I try to ignore it, but it sucks.

"You want what they have, don't you?" Lucy asks walking up beside me.

"Sounds as if you have it," I say, taking one of the chips from the bowl and popping it in my mouth.

"Not really. We're just kind of talking and getting to know each other," she shrugs her shoulders, but I can see what Faith means. There's definitely more to the story that she's not sharing.

We all file into the sunroom. If I hadn't seen it attached to Lexi's house with my own eyes, I would believe it belongs to someone else. While the rest of Lexi's house has a beautiful farmhouse style with neutral colors, this sunroom is colorful with hot pops of colors everywhere you look.

"This is my fun room. I love coming out here to read or relax, especially when the weather is nice." Lexi says, taking my arm and guiding me to sit down next to her on one of the sofas.

"Okay, here are girls' night rules," Lexi says. She holds up one finger. "One. No drinking and driving. There are guest bedrooms upstairs and downstairs and couches around the house. Crash anywhere you want. You are always welcome."

She holds up a second finger. "Two, we are friends first. We are not boss and employees. Here we are friends. Venting about work is okay, venting about patients is okay, and venting about guys is encouraged. We are here to support each other," she says.

Then she holds up a third finger. "Three. What is talked about at girls' night stays at girls' night. This is a safe place. What is talked about in this room doesn't leave this room. Got it?"

Once Lexi has gone over the rules, everyone digs into their food, and for the first few minutes, it's quiet.

Kaitlyn says to us, "I'll begin. Apparently, my dad is dating someone, and he posted about it on social media. But first, let's take a moment and collectively agree how weird it is my dad is telling everyone about his dating life on social media. Then, I guess my stepmom saw it, and went ballistic. She didn't even get alimony in the divorce because of all the crap that she put my dad through. Now Dad has a restraining order and a no contact order on her." Kaitlyn finishes, shoving more food in her mouth.

If this is how girls' night starts, I will be thoroughly entertained and will definitely be back.

"We all know your stepmom is psycho. I think the bigger thing here is how are you feeling about your dad's dating life?" Lexi asks her.

"I felt fine about it until it was all over social media. They are great together. Not only is she really nice, but she's also a fantastic cook. I just don't want to log on to social media and see pictures of them kissing, filling my feed."

"So unfollow him, and you won't see his stuff unless you specifically go to his profile," Mandy says.

"What? You can do that?" Kaitlyn asks, her eyes going wide.

Immediately, she goes and sits by Mandy, pulling out her phone and they huddle over it for a few minutes.

"You are a lifesaver," Kaitlyn says before coming back to her spot at the other end of the couch.

"How are you living the mom life?" Lauren asks Lexi.

"I'm loving every minute of it, but I'm exhausted," Lexi says with a winsome smile on her face.

"I remember those early years. Mine's in school now and I can honestly say it's just a different kind of exhausted," Lauren says.

That sounds very familiar as I remember my sister saying the exact same thing.

The night goes on and just about everyone has something to say. Life updates, family updates, personal updates, they share it all.

Time and time again, I watch these ladies build each other up and help solve their problems.

And it finally gives me the courage to speak up.

"So I..."

I stop when all eyes in the room turn to me. It's now or never and I don't want to chicken out since I could really use some advice.

"There's this guy," I start and everyone smiles.

"There's always a guy. Do we know him?" Paisley asks.

Lexi knows who I'm talking about, and I'm pretty sure Kaitlyn does too, as does Faith, so there really is no point in beating around the bush.

"Yeah, it's Zane," I say. Then immediately feel my face turn bright red.The girls clap and giggle, genuinely excited for me.

"Okay, girls, let's hear her out," Lexi says, trying to get them to calm down.

"Well, I want to start off by saying he's a really good guy. The problem is, it's a lot of little things. He's more than ten years older than me, and that seems to bother him. Then, as you can guess, the fact that he's still learning how to communicate with the world seems to be a crutch that he leans on. Not that I can blame him. Even though it's made communicating difficult, we're doing it, and we're learning." I stop to take a breath.

"But," Lexi encourages me on.

"But then there are some larger issues. Such as I've always wanted to have a family, and he's never wanted kids," I say, unsure of how much I plan on opening up about this topic.

"Men change their minds on that all the time once they fall in love. Then they start picturing the future, and it's always with children and with the woman that they love. Don't let that stop you from moving forward. I guarantee you it won't be an issue later." Mandy encourages me and voices ring out in agreement.

"But there's something else, isn't there?" Kassi says, studying my face and speaking up for the first time.

"I can't have kids. I was in a car accident a couple of years ago and it was pretty bad. I lost a lot of blood and was hemorrhaging because there was part of a tree lodged in my abdomen. When they couldn't stop the bleeding, they had to remove my uterus to save my life. So, at least physically I cannot have children."

"Does he know that?" Lexi asks.

"Yeah, I told him and I'm worried that the fact that I can't have kids is what's kept him from running, since he doesn't want them anyway. But I still want a family someday. Though I won't be going the traditional route. I'm enjoying spending time with him, and I feel like he's starting to open up and talk about his hopes and dreams a little more. But I also don't want to do anything to set his progress back."

"First of all, you are talking of putting his needs above yours just because you think it's going to set back his progress if you don't. The men and women here are going to have the setbacks that life is going to give them. We don't want them to be in such a cocoon that they don't know how to deal with real life when they leave," Kaitlyn says, with everyone agreeing.

"It sounds more like you really like him, but you're not ready to walk away even though some part of you is saying that you should. We can give you the whole listen to your heart BS and everything, but when it comes down to it, the only one who can make that decision is you. You're the one who knows what's best for you. Sometimes life will step in the way and force our hand," Lauren says.

I get a sense that she's more experienced with it than I realized.

"It sounds like you're in a situationship and have to see where the cards fall," Kassi says.

"What the hell is a situationship?" Lexi asks.

"It's kind of like friends with benefits, but you don't have to be sleeping together. It's all the makings of a relationship, but it doesn't have an official title. You're just kind of waiting for the other one to say, hey, I want this," Kassi explains.

"Never been happier to be married," Lexi says.

All the married women chime in with head nods and 'yesses.'

We spend the rest of the night talking about fun stuff, celebrity gossip, things happening around town, and anything that pops up. It's fun and relaxing, and something that I didn't know I needed.

After a while, we all start heading back to the kitchen, and everyone but me goes to their guys.

Being the only single one there, I duck out pretty fast, not wanting to be a third wheel.

They definitely gave me a lot to think about.

CHAPTER 10

CARLEE

I'm having dinner with my sister, Brian, and Liz because because they're leaving town tomorrow to visit his mom who is in the hospital. Apparently, she and his dad can no longer live alone since she fell and broke her hip, so they are getting ready to move them into an assisted leaving facility.

Brian in an only child and his parents had him later in life. He is their miracle baby after being told they would never have children. So, it's all on him to take care of his parents, and I know my sister will be right there by his side.

During the week while I work, Liz will be staying with my parents since she has school. Then on the weekend, she will spend it with me.

"So, you think a week will be enough time?" I ask them over dinner.

"We honestly don't know," Brian says. "I think moving Dad in will be easy. Then Mom will go there right from the hospital, but the hard part is taking care of their house. Deciding what they will take with them is a top priority. Dad says he's been packing and sorting, but I won't know if that's true until we get there."

I can see the worry and stress all over his face. I know they hate to be apart from Liz, and I know this can't be easy on him.

"Well, you take all the time you need. Liz and I will have so much fun, she won't even realize how long you are gone. And if you need anything, I am but a phone call away. I can be up there in a few hours to help pack, move, cook dinner, whatever you need. Plus, I made some friends that have hulking ex-military husbands who I'm sure wouldn't need much convincing to come help out."

"Oh yeah, the girls' night. Tell me about it!" My sister changes the subject, and I let her. It's obvious that they both need a distraction.

"It was nice. I was the only single one there, but all the girls have the kind of relationship with their guys that the two of you have. We had fried chicken sliders, and all the sides you'd have at a BQ like potato salad, Cole slaw, baked beans, and cornbread. Several of us brought dessert. I made your brownie recipe, and it was gone so fast." I smile, remembering how everyone gushed about the brownies.

"You know I didn't mean the food!" my sister laughs.

"Well, I wanted to hear about the food," Liz says, giggling.

"I would go back for the food alone," I say to my niece.

"Carlee!" My sister screeches exasperatedly.

"Okay, okay. Everyone there accepted me from the start. They all talked about everything from kids to their relationships, family, and updates on stuff that had been discussed before. Then I got some good old fashioned liquid courage and brought up Zane. I told them everything that I told you the other night. It's like now that I told you it just comes pouring out of me. They were so supportive and understanding and offered some good advice about talking to him and being open. Then one girl said I was in a situationship and that finally put it all in perspective."

"What is a situationship?" Liz asks.

"It's where you are maybe dating or simply talking to someone. While you are doing all the relationship things, but you two aren't committed to each other. You aren't boyfriend and girlfriend," I clarify.

"Well, that's stupid," she says.

"Hey, we don't use that word," Brian says sternly.

"I'm sorry, but it is. Aunt Carlee you need to talk to him. Tell him to either lock it down with you or you will move on to the next guy because you are a great catch and deserve better," Liz says with so much confidence and encouragement, I'm moved.

"Lord, I wish it was that easy," I say with a halfhearted laugh.

"Honestly, I agree with her." My sister says just as Mom and Dad burst through the front door.

"I really wish they would knock," Brian mumbles, but we all laugh.

"We are back here finishing up dinner," my sister yells.

It's no secret and we all know my parents are a bit much. My sister and Brian have come to my aid against my mother many times. They keep telling me to stand up for myself yet know how hard that is for me, so they step in when needed. Maybe one day I will be assertive and be confident with her, but until then I just keep my head down.

When Mom and Dad join us in the dining room, we greet them with smiles and hugs as they get seated.

"I brought my banana pudding for dessert. I'm just sorry we couldn't make dinner. If we had more notice, we could have moved our plans, but Steve and Shirley were only in town for a few days, and they leave tomorrow," Mom says.

"It's fine, Mom. We understand. It's not like we could plan for Brian's mom to take a fall at a time that was convenient for you," my sister sasses, smiling.

She gets away with it because she is married and has a child. If I said that, Mom would go on a ten-minute rant about how men don't want sassy women and I'd die alone.

"I love your banana pudding, Mom. Maybe one day you will trust me with the recipe," I say, trying to switch topics.

Mom's eyes shoot over to me like she forgot I was there.

"Until you tie down a man, you shouldn't be eating dessert. Men don't like curves. When you manage to get a guy who wants to marry you, I might give you the recipe as a wedding gift."

"Mom! That was so rude. What is wrong with you?" My sister says, angrily.

"I'm sorry. I'm just worried about her." Mom says it as if I'm not even in the room. "If she waits too long, she will miss her window to have kids."

"Mom, I'm twenty-two. I still have over a decade to have kids." I stumble over my words as my sister gives me a look. I know she is trying to communicate that now is the perfect time to tell Mom and Dad what is going on, but I just give my head a slight shake.

The last thing I want is to get into this now when she and Brian are getting ready to leave town. Liz will have to deal with the aftermath when she goes home with them tonight.

"You know, I really thought college would be a good place for you to meet your future husband. Are you sure that Eric boy won't take you back? He was so nice," Mom says.

"That's enough, dear," Dad says with a pointed look at my mom.

"Mom, he didn't call you when I was in the hospital fighting for my life. That's what you consider nice? Have you lost your mind?" I snap, standing up to storm out of here.

"What are you doing? We just got here!" Mom says.

"I have to side with Carlee on this one. That was over the line," Brian says.

I'm shocked because he always stays out of it.

"Agreed," my sister says.

"I'm going. I need to get ready for my art therapy class tomorrow. Call me to let me know you made it in," I say, hugging my sister and Brian.

"Liz, I will see you in two days."

Then I kiss my dad on the cheek and don't say a word. Without so much as a look in my mom's direction, I leave. Normally, her words don't bother me so badly and I don't stick up for myself like I just did. But it seems the more people I tell and who I know are on my side, the more of a backbone I have.

CHAPTER 11

ZANE

When I find her in the garden today, Carlee seems different. She is sitting on the swing, staring off into space. Normally, her head is buried in her sketchbook, but today, her mind is anywhere but here.

Since hasn't seen me, I take a moment to observe her. There is definitely something on her mind, but it doesn't affect her prettiness. She still looks more beautiful than my mind can remember when I think of her at night. She has that girl next door vibe going on. With her, what you see is what you get. She doesn't wear a ton of makeup, and her glossy brown hair is either down or in a messy bun, and it's both natural and appealing.

Making my way over to her, she doesn't even realize I'm there. When I sit on the swing making it move, she jumps, obviously startled. Then when she finally notices me, she looks at me with those wide amber eyes and a big smile.

Are you okay? I ask.

I don't know. She sets her sketchbook down by her side.

Want to talk about it? I'm hoping she says yes because whatever it is, I want to help her through it.

I had dinner at my sister's last night, and things were good. Today, they left to check on her husband's mother. He's an only child, and his mom fell and broke her hip, and now he's moving them to assisted living. There are a lot of things both my sister and Brian will have to deal with, like the house and getting them moved. My niece is going to stay with Mom and Dad during the school week and with me on weekends until they get back.

Dinner was peaceful and fun until my mom shows up for dessert.

She pauses and I instantly know whatever is going on in her head has to do with her mom. I haven't met the woman, but I know what Carlee has told me and her mom sounds like a real piece of work just like my dad. The problem is, I walked away and never looked back. Though she seems to have more trouble cutting those ties.

Reaching out, I take her hand in mine, trying to offer her comfort while she gathers her thoughts.

My mom brought her banana pudding, which I love. When I wanted some, she was hurtful and mean. She told me that I don't need dessert if I plan to catch a husband and maybe she will give me the recipe at my wedding. As if that wasn't enough, she went on about how I should crawl back to Eric. I lost it. My sister lost it. Even Brian said something to her. How can she want me back with someone who left me in a hospital fighting for my life and never bothered to even call my family?

At this point, there are tears in her eyes, so I put my arm around her, pulling her into me. Wrapping her in a hug, holding her close to me, I wish more than anything I could protect her from the outside world. That I could stop all the pain she was in and keep her from ever getting hurt again. But this is a battle she has to fight herself, and I have to support her from the sidelines. However, it doesn't make it any easier.

Last night I think it really sank in that she doesn't care for ME just what I can give HER aka grandkids. I left without saying a word to her and didn't even say goodbye. I don't know what happened after I told my sister I'd talk to her tonight. When I go to pick up Liz for the weekend, I will have to face my mother.

While I hate she is being treated like this, do I really have a foot to stand on to defend her? I want to. I want to be the one who stands up for her and shields her from people like this. I don't care who it is, even if it's her own family.

I ask, wanting to see where her head is. *How do you feel about it all?*

Honestly, it felt good telling her what I thought. But then I felt bad about liking how it felt. She's my mom. I know how she treats me isn't okay, and it certainly isn't normal. I know it, but she is still my mom, and it's so hard to walk away from her. You know?

I get it. It was easier for me because by the time I left for boot camp, my dad had pushed me past my limit.

Silently, we sit there in the garden, soaking up the beauty and peace. She rests her head on my shoulder, and I pull her to my side. Right now in this place, I can shield her from the world and give her some comfort.

As I take in the garden around me, I keep my eyes toward the garden entrance making sure no one disrupts the peace Carlee so desperately needs.

Tell me about your family? she asks.

I guess she wants to take her mind off it all and I can't blame her. I debate what I should say. Telling her the truth about my family seems like a bad idea. It's the wrong time because she is looking for a distraction, not something sad. So I go for a funny story instead.

My dad loved to fish. He runs a fishing charter company, and he was looking for me to take over. That's another story. But the first time he took me out fishing on a charter with him, I was ten. We would go fishing around town all the time, but this was the first time I was allowed on the boat with him during a paid charter. I felt twenty feet tall.

Pausing, I am remembering that day clearly. It's the day that changed everything, but at the same time I still laugh every time I remember it.

As soon as we are leaving the harbor, the fishermen start drinking. So by the time we reach our spot to fish, they have had a few. I helped them bait their hooks and get them all set up. I felt so important. Once they were ready to go, my dad asked me if I wanted to put a line in the water with him at the front of the boat. Of course, I said yes.

I'm smiling, remembering the way the sun hit my skin that day and the look on my dad's face as I helped bait all their hooks.

At this point I'm smiling from ear to ear, lost in the memory.

Well, the day goes on, and more drinking happens, of course. By the time my hook gets a bite, I'm struggling to reel it in. So my dad is helping, and the guys who hired him are grabbing nets and leaning over to try to get the fish. They had too much to drink and fell in. My dad fell in, trying to pull them back in, and then started yelling at me.

Carlee sits up, looking at me with her eyes sparkling. *What did you do?*

I jumped in the water because I didn't want to be the only one not swimming.

This causes her to burst in to laughter. Fuck, what I wouldn't give to hear that laugh. To know what she sounds like. But just the fact that I'm the one who made her laugh does something funny inside my chest.

Still laughing, she is leaning closer to me, pulling me in to her. Already so close, I don't want to lose this opportunity, so I rest my head on her forehead, soaking her in. She still has a smile on her face as she looks up at me. Whatever that look that's in her eyes, and the way she smiles teasingly, makes me come undone.

Before I know it, my lips are on hers. She lets out a small gasp and then she is kissing me back. Tangling my hands in her hair, I use them to angle her head to deepen the kiss.

She tastes like cherry chapstick and innocence and an indefinable something I want more than anything. When she moans into the kiss and places her hand on my waist, I know this girl is mine.

There is no evading it. I need to stop using all those excuses on why we can't work and show her we can. Every day, I'll show her how perfect we are together. How we need each other.

I'm not going to lie. I've kissed many women, but this one? It's unlike anything I've ever experienced. My heart is racing, my cock is hard, and all I want is more. While the last thing I want to do is end this kiss, I'm also aware we are in a public space, so I reluctantly pull away.

She is breathing as hard as I am and her lips are slightly swollen and her cheeks are flushed.

Yeah, I'm pretty proud that I put that look on her. It's never mattered to me before.

This woman has wormed her way through my walls and into my heart. She doesn't even know it.

But that kiss? It's sealed her fate. She is mine and there is no going back now.

CHAPTER 12

CARLEE

That kiss.

I can't even form words because it short-circuited my brain.

After our time together, walking back in to Oakside so he could go to his appointment was difficult. All I wanted was for him to stay and keep kissing me. Though honestly, I didn't want to make out with him where everyone could see and watch us.

Once he went to his appointment, I took off downstairs to Lexi's office. When I got there, Paisley was sitting on the couch and Lexi was at her desk chair, talking about a patient.

"Well, I will leave you two alone," Paisley said, standing when she saw me at the door.

"Actually, I could use your advice too. If you have time?" I want to include her because I really like her.

From what I've observed, she is sweet, kind, and caring. She is also a very bubbly person and I can't help but smile when I'm around her.

"I can stay," she says, sitting down on the couch. It's no accident Lexi purchased it for her office. It's a soft tan microfiber couch that is so comfortable that nobody ever wants to get up.

"This is about Zane, isn't it?" Lexi says.

"How did you know?" I ask, shocked she can read me so well.

"I know you two just came in from the garden. I have eyes everywhere," she jokes.

"Did your eyes tell you that he kissed me? I mean, he *kissed* me." I say and both women's jaws drop.

"Seriously!" they ask in unison.

"Yep." I nod, smiling as I remember that kiss. Wow! Now that was a kiss I know I will never forget. It's the kind of kiss I will be sitting on my front porch watching my grandkids playing in the yard and still be thinking about.

"Okay, start at the beginning," Lexi says as she pulls her chair across the room so she's next to the couch.

"Well, I was in the garden on the swing when he joined me. Though I was so lost in thought over the family dinner we had last night that he startled me."

"What happened at your family dinner?" Paisley asks.

I give them the short version of what my mom said and how my sister stood up for me and so did her husband. Then I tell them about how I left without even acknowledging my mom.

"Good for you, standing up for yourself. I know it wasn't easy, but it had to feel empowering," Lexi says.

"That's the thing. It felt great last night. Then today I doubt everything. After all, she is my mom," I admit.

"Just because they are family doesn't mean they can't be toxic to you and your peace. You have to set boundaries with people like that or it will affect you in many ways." Paisley advises me.

"I'm really starting to understand that," I sigh. "Anyway, I told Zane all this, and he pulled me into his arms and we cuddled. It did make me feel better. Then I asked him to tell me about his family. He told me a fishing story about a time out with his dad. It was funny, and we both laughed together. But it seemed to trigger him. He put his forehead on mine and the next thing I knew, we were kissing."

"Good kiss? Short?" Lexi asks.

"Amazing kiss, deep and pretty long. By the time we pulled apart, he had to come in for his appointment."

Both girls squeal like teenagers, and then sigh.

"I knew he liked you like that. The kiss proves it." Lexi nods sagely.

"Well, I like him too. But that still doesn't resolve the matter that I want kids and he doesn't. Even though I'm not able to have kids, adoption has been something I've been thinking about. From what I've heard from him, I don't think that's even on the table."

"You need to talk to him. You can make all the assumptions you want, but none of it means anything until you hear his thoughts," Paisley says.

"I know. Just seems my brain forgets that any time he is around."

"Yeah, I know that feeling. Easton had that effect on me. He still does. I'll just stare at him and my mind will go blank." Paisley giggles.

"What if kids are a deal breaker for him? That's what I'm worried about. Do I give up my dream of children for the right guy?" I ask.

"The right guy won't make you give up your dream. He will be right there with you to adopt or go wherever you journey to become a mom takes you. Through it all, he'll support you and be at your side. Don't settle because the right man won't make you," Lexi says.

"I agree. But also I think men don't always picture themselves as a dad. Especially at Zane's age. With everything going on in his life, children aren't even on his radar. But when guys find the right woman, they see a future and it starts to include children. So I wouldn't write him off just yet. Take it slow and see where it goes," Paisley adds.

"Thanks guys. I have a lot to think about. Now I need to get going, so I can get my guest room set up. My niece is staying with me this weekend and she wants to have a painting party where I teach her to paint. Oh, and there has to be cake. Her words," I say.

"That sounds like so much fun. Maybe we can do our own paint and sip class one girls' night. You can teach us to paint something easy. We'll have drinks and dessert. It could be really entertaining," Paisley says.

"Let's do it. Just let me know when," I say.

"Sounds good. I'll talk to the other girls and get it set up," Lexi says.

As I head home, the whole time my mind on that kiss. By the time I get there, I'm so damn turned on I know I won't be able to concentrate on anything else if I don't get some relief. Going straight to my bedroom, I close the door, making sure the curtains are closed, and strip down to my bra and underwear. Then I crawl into bed.

I pull my vibrator out of my nightstand and lie in bed. Then I think of that kiss again. Though I don't think it's going to take much to push me over the edge. Turning my vibrator on, I slide my panties down and put the vibrator between my legs.

Then I fantasize about how hot it made and also, what if it had happened in his room instead. If we didn't have to stop. Taking my time, I imagine that he's kissing down my neck and running a hand up under my shirt to play with my nipples that are as hard as diamonds. Or maybe he would reach down and found out how wet I am.

The vibrator keeps ramping things up and every muscle in my body tightens. What I wouldn't give to hear him groan when we finds out I'm soaking wet for him. What would it feel like to have one of his thick fingers slide inside me? I kick the vibrator up to the next speed. That's enough to push me over the edge.

My orgasm hits me hard and fast, making me groan. Once the pleasure has passed, I shut the vibrator off and lay there drained. I feel relief for the first time since the kiss.

That is until I start thinking about the kiss again, and then I'm turned on all over again. I groan because this is going to be a long night. If I'm this turned on from a kiss, what would happen if we actually had sex?

I'm not sure if I want to find out, but my body sure as hell wants to.

CHAPTER 13

ZANE

I haven't been able to stop thinking about that kiss. It's been on my mind and I haven't been able to see Carlee since then. I have no idea where her head is on it. It's raining today so I have a feeling she is somewhere inside, but I know she is here because she has an art therapy class later this afternoon.

When I check out the room she has been using as a studio, I find her alone in there painting. Her back is to the door, so I stand there watching her, trying not to make a sound and distract her.

It's obvious she is in the zone and completely into her painting of what looks like a farmhouse on a plot of land with some hills.

Every stroke of her brush has me mesmerized. It's amazing how she makes a picture appear from imagining it in her head. When she pauses and stares off to space, I wonder if she is seeing the finished picture in her mind's eye. All of a sudden, I can't stand to not be closer to her, so I knock on the door frame. She turns to look at me and smiles a welcome to me.

Slowly, I make my way up to where she is at the front of the room.

What are you painting? I ask.

It's silly. This one is just for me, she says, shaking her head and putting everything away.

It's not silly. Tell me. Reaching out, I take her hand and stop her from moving around the room.

It's my dream house. It's actually about thirty minutes from here. Every now and then on my way to one of my favorite art galleries, I pass by it.

I step forward to look at the painting through new eyes. It's a white square farmhouse with a wrap-around porch and a porch swing at one end. The house overlooks an enormous expanse of land with cows and horses grazing. A vegetable garden is off to one side and wildflowers cover the hill in the background. At the far end, there is a group of trees, making it look like the perfect place to spend a lazy weekend. Perfect to raise kids.

A pang hits me because that is what she wants more than anything.

Children.

I don't know how to give that to her. I didn't have the best example of a family growing up, so I'm not sure what kind of father I could be. Also, knowing my crappy home life, would she even want me to be a parental figure in her kid's lives? But damn if I can let her go.

It's beautiful. Peaceful, I say.

Yes, she says. *I can picture myself sitting on the porch painting. Or sitting in the swing watching a storm roll in while reading.*

As she describes it, I can see it. Me curled up with her on that swing, maybe with a dog at our feet. Fuck, if I don't want that with her more than I should.

Imagine the painting that would come out of it. You will do it one day. I know you will. I tell her and send a silent prayer that maybe I can be the one by her side when she does it. Though I don't know how to get us there.

One day at a time. I just keep reminding myself. Right now, I don't need all the answers. Just remind myself to take life one day at a time.

So how has your day been so far? She asks, trying to change the subject.

I had my monthly testing. They checked my hearing to see if there is any improvement.

After the first time, I learned not to get my hopes up. I'd rather live with this and know this is my life now, than to get my hopes up each time I go in for testing, only to get disappointed when the tests show no improvements.

What did they say? She asks, though I can tell she is trying to keep her emotions out of it.

Still the same. They still have hope something might change, but I don't. It's not something I want, to be disappointed over and over again. I'd rather go in one day and be shocked there is a change, I say.

That makes sense. I can't imagine getting my hopes up each month only for them to be crushed. Oh, that's my phone. Hang on. She picks her phone up from the table next to her easel.

I can't tell what she is saying. Maybe I'll learn how to read lips after I master sign language. I like knowing what people are saying around me when they think I don't have a clue.

When she hangs up, she turns back to me.

That was Noah. Due to the weather and some of the delays with other appointments today he suggested we cancel the class and move it to tomorrow. I agreed. So do you have any plans today because I'm suddenly free?

Well, I'm sure we can find some trouble to get into. Want to head back to my room? Rainy days are great for watching a movie, I say. Really what I'm thinking is it's a way to get her alone and spend some time with her.

That sounds perfect. Let me clean up. She says with a smile.

What can I do to help? She puts me to work cleaning brushes while she puts the paints away and sets her canvas up to dry. Then after wiping down the counters and sink, she makes sure all the lights are turned off.

I take her hand in mine and lead her from the room, through the lobby and upstairs to my room, closing the door behind us. Immediately, she goes over to the couch and slips off her shoes, curling into a ball. I have to say she looks right at home, like she has always belonged there.

For the first time, it hits me how well she fits into my life. Even with all the changes going on in it right now, it's as if she was made for me. On instinct, I lock the door before I join her on the couch. She snuggles right up to my side.

What do you feel like watching? I ask.

Maybe something funny?

What do you normally watch when it's just you? I ask because I have a feeling it's something she doesn't think I will like.

Romantic movies, Rom-Coms, comedy. Nothing too serious. I like to laugh while watching TV.

Of course she does. This ball of sunshine doesn't want the darker things. But does she realize that my darker side comes as part of the package deal?

I put on a rom-com that she gets excited about. Even though there are captions, my mind wonders until she wraps her arm around me, holding me to her like I'm her favorite snuggly things.

When she looks up at me to make sure I'm still watching TV, I'm gone. I lean in and kiss her. She moves into me, letting a small moan escape as she wraps her arms around my neck. The next thing I know she is straddling my lap, her core pressed against my hard cock and I want nothing more than to lay her on the bed and have my way with her.

When she slowly starts grinding against me, my hands go to her hips and stop her. I pull back and lock eyes with her.

You can't tease me like that. It makes me want you in ways that require us moving to the bed. I'm hoping she will get the hint.

Then take me to the bed, she says without missing a beat.

Wrapping my arms tightly around her, I stand with her legs and arms wrapped around me and make my way to the bed and gently lay her down. After taking off my shoes, I climb in with her.

She looks so pretty lying in my bed with her long hair on my pillow. Suddenly she looks shy.

I haven't... I haven't been with anyone since my accident, she says

I instantly get her meaning. She has scars from it, I'm sure. Just like I have new scars that no one has seen yet.

Do you want this? Because I want you more than my next breath and a few scars aren't going to scare me away because I've got some of my own to match, I say.

I want this, and I want you. I have for a while now, she says.

Well, game on. Before I do anything, I want to feel her lips on mine and enjoy this moment before everything changes. When I remove my shirt, her jaw drops as she takes me in. It's hard to sit here and let her look, but if I want her to be comfortable, I need to do this before I take it any further.

After she takes me in, she sits up and reaches out to touch my skin. The sizzle between us is electrifying. Then, instead of tracing my scars, she traces my tattoos, which cover my arms and chest. When she begins kissing one of my scars, a shiver racks my body. I can't wait another minute to see her gorgeous body. I reach for her shirt and she lets me pull it off her. She is in a plain tan lace bra and her pale skin prickles with goose bumps. I remove the bra and it lands on the floor in the growing pile of clothes.

Her breasts are perky, and her nipples are waiting to be nibbled or licked. But before I move to them, I see the pink scars across her belly. Some are straight that look to be from the surgery and some are jagged and twisted that must be from the accident. I run my tongue over each one as my hand undoes the button of her shorts so I can see the entire scar. She lifts her bottom and I slide the shorts down and off her, tossing them aside.

You're beautiful, I say, looking into her eyes. *These scars remind me of all you have been through and all that you fought through. They are the best part of you. And after we do this, you will be mine.* I tell her as the tears well in her eyes.

Unable to watch her shed a single tear, I kiss her like I need air to breathe. Our kiss becomes like a volcano, hot, hurried, and frantic. We can't seem to get close enough to each other. She tugs at my jeans and before I know it, they are gone and I'm in my boxer briefs and she is in a tiny pair of lace panties.

You sure you want this? I ask one more time.

More than anything.

Standing, I pull my underwear off and my cock springs free. Her eyes go wide. I'm not a small guy in that department and if she hasn't been with anyone since her ex she only has one person to compare me to. I get the idea that he was small in more ways than one.

I grab a condom from the nightstand. Never so glad Noah put a few in there just in case he said. In record time, I've got the condom on.

Then I climb back into bed and kiss my way up her legs to her panties before slowly pulling them off and tossing them aside.

When I get to her center, I pull her legs apart and find her soaking wet. Fuck, she is perfect. I don't hesitate before diving in for my first taste of her. Fuck, is she sweet. I'm instantly addicted.

Her hands grip my hair and hold me in a place which makes me determined to hear her cries as I play with her.

Taking two fingers, I slide them slowly into her as my tongue keeps working on her clit. What I wouldn't give to hear her moans right now and to hear what she sounds like when she comes. But I know she's close because her thighs are gripping the side of my head tightly and her body is tensing up.

When her pussy constricts to a death grip on my fingers, I can tell she's coming. Knowing I was the one to make her is a feeling that soothes my soul.

When she starts to relax, I'm satisfied to see she's flushed with a smile in her face.

Even though my cock is hard and yelling at me, I want to stay in this moment as long as I can.

Finally, not wanting to wait any longer, I kiss my way up her body before my lips land on hers. She wraps her arms around my neck, holding me to her.

I'm settled between her legs, with my cock nestled at her entrance, while enjoying the feel of her curvy body pressed against me. But it seems my girl is a bit more impatient. She wraps her legs around my waist and digs her heels into my ass, pushing the tip of my cock into her.

Taking the hint, I slowly slide into her. Her eyes close and her head tilts back. Then I pull out and thrust back in again and again until I bottom out inside her.

For a moment, I rest my head on her shoulder because fuck she feels so amazing and I want to remember this. But what I really want is to tell her that. Lord, the things I'd tell her if I could speak right now.

Gaining momentum, my cock is drilling into her wet pussy. She clutches me tightly, opens her eyes, and they land on mine. Our eyes lock and it's like we are saying everything we want to tell each other, but can't say. I keep a steady pace and she meets each of my thrusts. Picking up my speed, her eyes start to close. Desperate for that connection again, and needing her eyes on me, I touch the side of her cheek. Once she understands, she opens them, looking at me with passion.

Her pussy starts to flutter around me and fuck, I want to tell her to come on my cock like the good girl she is. But the better use of my hands is reaching between us and stoking her clit, causing her body to tense as her orgasm builds. Her pussy has a vise grip on my cock and pulls my cum from me harder than I thought possible. By the time I'm done cumming, her body is relaxed and she's got a smile lighting up her face. I collapse beside her and pull her into my arms.

Her body fits perfectly against mine and I know this is where she is meant to be. Holding her tightly, I kiss the top of her head as she snuggles into me. I want to lie here forever, but our beautiful moment is broken when her body tenses and she pulls out of my arms and looks over at her phone.

CHAPTER 14

CARLEE

I don't know how life can get any better. I just spent the weekend with my niece and we had a blast. Our painting party was complete with a cake we baked together. After doing each other's nails, we watched Disney movies all weekend from a fort we built in the living room.

Basically, all the things my parents wouldn't let us do growing up. Liz and I had fun and I can't wait to do it again.

Then to come back to Oakside and despite the weather being lousy and my class having to be canceled, I had one of the best days I never expected with Zane.

Who would think that watching a movie would turn into the best sex of my life? But it did, and as we lie in his bed together, I felt safe. Not wanting the trance to be broken, but my phone is ringing and I know I need to see who is calling. When I see it's Mom, I ignore it. Whatever she has to say, I don't want to hear it.

But when my dad calls back immediately after, I know something is wrong.

It's my dad. I say to Zane before I answer the call.

"Dad?" I ask, sitting up and starting to get dressed. While I'm talking to my father, I can't be sitting here naked. Even though I know he can't see me, I just can't do it.

"Sweetheart." His voice is broken in a way I've never heard before in my life and instantly I know whatever he is going to tell me isn't going to be good.

"What is it?" I freeze, waiting for what I'm sure is bad news.

"There was an accident. Kaylee and Brian were hit by a drunk driver," he says, his voice breaking.

"Okay. What hospital have they been taken to? Let's get there and I can sit with Liz while you go see them." My mind is racing and I'm planning all the logistics.

"We need you to come get Liz right now. We are packing and from what we are told it's not something Liz needs to see. When it's time, you can bring her." Dad is more composed now, and I'm relieved.

"I'm on my way. I'll be there in twenty minutes," I say, racing to put on my clothes. Hanging up, I look at Zane, who is watching me with anxiety.

Family emergency. I have to go get my niece," I say not sure what else to tell him.

He nods, walking over to me and pulls me into his arms. His embrace is calming and exactly what I need right now. Taking a deep, shuddering breath, I reluctantly pull away. While I don't want to move out of his comforting and safe arms, I have to get going. Zane grabs me for a quick kiss.

Let me know if you need anything. I mean that, he says.

Nodding, I finish getting dressed. Then I pull him in for another quick kiss before I'm out the door.

I'm such a mess praying everything is okay, that I don't even see Lexi when I hit the lobby until she stands right in front of me.

"Carlee, are you okay?" She places her hands on my shoulders.

"My sister was in a car accident. I need to go get my niece so my parents can go to my sister," I say.

"Oh shit. You are in no condition to drive. Let Noah drive you," she urges.

"No, I will need my car." At least I think I will.

"Listen, he will drive your car anywhere you need to go, and then I will come get him once you're home."

"I'm not taking no for an answer. You are in no state to drive." Noah says, walking to up me and taking my keys out of my hand.

"Are you sure?" I ask, not wanting to be a burden.

"Positive. You are a friend and we want to be there for you," Noah says.

"Thank you." I'm not used to this kind of support from people.

Lexi hugs me, and then Noah is helping me out to my car. It would be funny if I wasn't so stressed that when he climbs into the driver's seat, he is folded like a pretzel as he waits for the seat to slide slowly backward.

"Sorry, I know I'm short," I say.

"It's okay. Every time I get in the car after my wife drives it, I have to do the same thing. I'm used to it." He tells me, smiling. "So, where are we going?"

"My parents' house." After I give him directions, my thoughts run anxiously through my mind. Thankfully, he doesn't try to talk Instead he puts on the radio and leaves me to my worries.

When we pull into my parents' driveway, I pause when Noah starts to get out.

"Please, will you wait here? Trust me, with how my parents are, you will want to avoid it," I tell him.

"I've faced worse. I'm stuck to your side until things calm down. Lexi would murder me otherwise," he says.

"That might be kinder than my parents." But I don't try to stop him as he follows me up to their door.

Once I get there, I knock because this place hasn't felt like home in a really long time.

My mom opens the door with tears in her eyes, and seems startled when she sees Noah.

"This is not the time to bring home some stray guy. Carlee, what is wrong with you?"

I open my mouth to defend myself, but Noah beats me to it.

"Ma'am, my name in Noah Carr. Carlee is friends with my wife, Lexi. When she got the call, she was with us, and I decided to drive her because she was in no position to drive herself. I am strictly her to support here and your family," Noah says in a sweet voice that seems to calm my mom right down.

"Well, that is so nice. Come on in," Mom says.

No sooner do I step into the room, than Liz runs past everyone and right into my arms. I pick her up and she wraps her legs around my waist.

"This is my niece, Liz. Liz, this is my friend Noah," I say as tears fill my eyes.

"Here is Liz's bag. If she needs anything else, you have the key Kaylee's place." Dad tells me as walks up to us.

Noah takes the bag from my dad and introduced himself again.

"Our flight leaves in four hours, but we are going to leave now and wait at the airport," Mom says.

While I know it's only an hour's drive to the airport, it won't do any good sitting around here fussing.

"What happened?" I ask.

"After seeing his mom in the hospital, they were heading back to Brian's parents and were hit head on by a drink driver. Both of them are unconscious. That's all we know. We got the call because we were listed as an emergency contact in Kaylee's phone," Dad says.

"Okay, well, keep me updated. I will take care of Liz and as soon as you can, let us know and we'll come up and visit."

All the way to the car, Liz doesn't let go of me. Fortunately, Noah helps buckle her in and makes sure I'm in the car and buckled up before heading out. I give him directions to my house and by the time we get there, Liz is sound asleep.

"Let me help carry her in," Noah whispers and I nod, grateful for the help.

Noah follows me up to the house and waits as I unlock the door.

"Here, this way." I lead him down the hallway to the second door on the right. It's set up at my guest room, but really it was all Liz who decorated it, so it's really more her room anyway.

Noah lays her on the bed just as my phone rings.

"It's my dad," I say.

"Answer it. I'll take her shoes off and get her tucked into bed," Noah says.

I nod and step back into the living room.

"Dad?" I answer.

"Sweetheart," his voice is choked up and I can hear Mom wailing in the background. My heart sinks because I instantly know without him saying anything, it's not good. When his words reach my ears, my world shatters.

"Kaylee and Brian didn't make it. Brian died on the way to the hospital and Kaylee died on the operating table."

Whatever he says after that, I have no idea. Because the phone falls from my hand and a moment later, Noah is there. My throat hurts and I realize I'm screaming "No!" over and over again.

It isn't until I pick my head up from Noah's shoulder where there's a huge wet spot on his shirt from my tears that I see I woke up Liz. Her tear-filled eyes are staring at me in shock.

"Aunt Carlee?" she cries out.

I hold up my arms and she runs into them while Noah holds us both.

"I'm so sorry, baby. They didn't make it," I say as we both burst into sobs gathered there in Noah's arms.

CHAPTER 15

ZANE

It's been a week.

A week since I've talked to her.

A week since i had her in my arms.

A week since she has been at Oakside.

A week since I've been able to lay eyes on her.

A family emergency. That is what she told me, but I've heard not a word since. Yesterday I was pissed that she just dropped off the face of the Earth. Art therapy has been put on hold. Her painting room was closed and nothing has been touched.

Today, I'm worried. So when Noah steps in to check on me, I straight out confront him about it.

Where is Carlee? Is she okay? I ask.

When his face instantly fills with pain, I know in my gut something is wrong. Very wrong.

Don't lie to me. It's all over your face. Then I watch the war inside his head happen.

I know he's fighting the loyalty of respecting Carlee as an employee and probably their friend, but he also knows what she means to me.

Finally, Noah nods, saying, *That last time she was here, she got a call her sister was in a car accident. She was in no condition to drive, so I drove her to get her niece. By the time I got the two of them home, she got another call. It was devastating news. Her sister and her brother in law had both died. Since then, she has been taking care of her niece and making all the arrangements.*

It hits me like a ton of bricks, and I have to sit down. She has been hurting and here I was mad because she hadn't reached out. What an idiot I am. Of course, there was a good reason.

Take me to her please. I ask Noah.

I don't think that's a good idea.

She is in pain and hurting. I need to be there for her. That's my job. I stare Noah down.

We lock eyes for a moment, and finally he seems to understand that she is mine and by her side is where I belong.

Give me a few minutes. Let me see what I can do. Okay? he says.

I nod, getting ready to go because one way or another, I am going to her.

It seems like forever until Noah comes back to my room.

I talked to my wife. Today she is our running around getting Liz set up at her house. She is the one named in the will to take care of Liz. Lexi suggests we go tomorrow and I agree.

Even though I want to argue and complain, I know have to trust them. As much as I want to protect her, I also have to do what is best.

Okay. But we go early, right?

Noah agrees, leaving me with my thoughts.

My mind is racing with questions, and I need some answers. Knowing that Lexi is the one who could answer some of my immediate questions, I go to the lobby hoping to find her. Fortunately, she is behind the front desk. When I walk up, she looks up at me with a sad smile.

When is the funeral? I ask.

In three days.

I'm going to need something to wear, as I don't have anything here.

She looks surprised, as if she didn't think I'd be going. Why wouldn't I be? Carlee is mine. That means taking care of her, and being by her side on one of the hardest days of her life.

I'll make sure you have something to wear.

Thank you.

I go for a walk in the garden and let my mind wander. She is now responsible for her niece. Not only that, but she's lost the only family worth a damn, and her best friend all in one swoop. Why didn't she reach out to me, though? Why wouldn't she tell me?

The questions keep circling in my head and by the time I reach the swing in the garden, my brain in yelling the answer at me.

Because you told her you didn't want kids. She now has a young child in her life. When her entire life changed, she thought I wouldn't want her anymore. She must have thought that because she was now raising her niece, it would be a deal breaker.

With any other girl I had ever dated, yes it would have been. My decision was firm and set. I did not want to have kids, and I was certain of it. But with Carlee, now that she's raising her niece, it gives me vision and possibilities I never thought I'd have. Us raising her together in the farmhouse she painted comes to mind.

That night, my dreams are filled with Carlee and the small family we would have. The three of us are on the front porch of the farmhouse, a storm rolling in and Carlee laying on the swing with her head in my lap reading as I watch the storm. Her niece sitting on the ground next to a dog, playing with her pet, and having fun giving him treats.

I could imagine the three of us working in the garden and going horseback riding. It's so clear in my dream that I wake up disoriented, and admittedly a little disappointed. Though it was just a dream, but it felt so real, and so perfect and I want it.

More than my next breath, I want that family with her. I want it all.

CHAPTER 16

ZANE

At the crack of dawn, I am up and ready to go to Carlee. Suddenly, I'm seeing a whole life I never knew I needed. I go right to the dining room and eat. Then I wait in the lobby ready for when Noah gets here. Even though I suspect that seven-thirty a.m. is probably a little too early to go to Carlee, I'm ready anyway. I don't want to waste any time. When Noah walks into the lobby at eight thirty, he does a double take when he sees me, but then acknowledges me with a smile.

We will leave here at nine. I want to make sure her niece is at school before you show up. I also got you this phone. It's part of the plan for your recovery here, and it will make communication easier. It's up to her to give you her number, but mine, Easton's, and your doctor's numbers are already programmed in, he says, handing me the phone.

Right away, I know this phone will be a godsend. I'm excited that I'll be able text Carlee whenever I want. Having a way to contact her when she isn't here to make sure things are okay, will be a big relief.

Thank you. I tell him as he nods and goes off to check on things or whatever else he does.

At nine o'clock on the dot, he is back in the lobby.

Ready? he asks.

Nodding, I follow him out to his car.

Even though the drive is short, it seems to go on forever because every minute away from her is torture.

Once we pull into her driveway, Noah turns to me again.

I'll wait and make sure she lets you in. Then I'm going to get back to Oakside. Text me when you are ready to leave and I will come get you. No matter how long you stay here today, at night you *have to come back to Oakside. It's our policy,* he says.

All I can do is nod my head and stare at the front door. Until now, that she might not want me here didn't even cross my mind. But I'm here for her now and I'm not going anywhere. So I get out of the car, walk up to the front door and knock. A moment later, Carlee answers. She is in black cotton shorts and a t-shirt, with her hair pulled up in a messy bun. Though she doesn't have on any makeup, and she has bags under her eyes, she's never looked more beautiful. When she sees me, her eyes go wide in surprise. I know then she had no idea I was coming. I would have thought Noah or Lexi would have told her.

Noah told me what happened. If I had known, I would have been here sooner. But I'm here now.

She shakes her head but doesn't say anything.

Why didn't you tell me? I ask her.

Opening the door, she points to the couch. Before I sit, I give a nod to Noah who starts backing out of the driveway. Then I sit on the couch and wait for her to join me. But she doesn't sit next to me, instead she takes the chair by the couch. In more ways than one, I hate the distance between us.

If anything were to happen to them, my sister and brother-in-law named me to take care of Liz. Of course, I didn't even have to think about it. Though in my wildest dreams, I never thought it would happen. There is no question that I will raise her and care for her. But you said you never wanted kids and I'm now an instant family. I figured you wouldn't want any part of all this.

She starts rambling and only stops when I pick her up and place her on the couch with me.

I never said that I don't want kids. Just that I hadn't ever considered it. But when I learned you couldn't have kids, I didn't give it much more thought. When I talked with Noah last night and he told me about your niece, for the first time I really thought about it, I say, waiting to see her reaction.

What did you come up with?

Well, I saw you and me on the porch of that house you painted. Liz is there playing with a dog, as we all watch a storm roll in. The idea of a family with you is something I never knew I wanted, but now I want it with everything in me.

Hoping I'm not scaring her off by coming on too strong, yet I also don't want her to doubt where I stand either.

She doesn't say anything, so I keep going.

I want what I pictured and I want us, all of us, more than anything. Even though you should be with someone your own age, there is no way in hell I can let you go to find someone else. The thought of another man touching you makes me want to kill.

Her beautiful eyes go wide, then she smiles and kisses me. I soak her in. The feel of having her lips on me for the first time in a week soothes my soul and calms me in a way I never knew was possible.

You aren't too old for me. You are perfect because you are mine. She kisses me again, stroking my face with her fingers.

While I want nothing more than to sink into her and love on every inch of her body, I know that isn't what she needs right now. Her next words confirm my thinking.

I want to stay here and kiss you all day, but I have to clean up and get dinner going. While Liz is at school, I have to do my painting. Oh, and the laundry. Then she starts listing things.

Grabbing her hands, I stop her and wait until her eyes meet mine.

Baby, you need to rest. Go take a nap or a long hot bath. I can start laundry and do some cleaning. I can even start dinner because yes, I'm actually a decent cook. Let me take care of you please, I plead.

She smiles at me. *A nap sounds great and maybe a shower after.*

Standing her up, I point down the hallway.

Go get some rest and let me worry about this.

She nods, kisses my check and leaves me to my tasks. I look around and decide to start the laundry first. Once that is going, I head back to the living room and straighten things up. It's just messy and obviously a young kid lives here.

Next is the kitchen. After I get a load of dishes going, I check to see what she has food wise. Pulling out stuff for dinner, I put it in the slow cooker so it will be ready. Then I make a game plan for lunch because Carlee will need to eat when she gets up.

After switching out the laundry, I start another load. Seeing that there are towels in the dryer, I fold them and put them away. Then I sit down for a minute and look around. I need to give some thought to my future. Right now, I don't know what my life after the military is going to look like. I don't know what I'm going to do. But I know without a shadow of a doubt, it involves the people in this house and the woman sleeping down the hall.

CHAPTER 17

CARLEE

Until I laid down in bed, I didn't realize how badly I needed that break. I was asleep as soon as I hit the pillow, which is never something that happens for me. When I check the time, it's just after twelve, so I get up. Then I take a nice hot shower, washing my hair and scrubbing every inch of my body and even shave, something I haven't done all week.

I dress in something more flattering than the shorts and shirt I went to bed in and go to find Zane. The house is quiet and I don't want to sneak up on him and scare him. But when I get to the living room, I see it's cleaned up, so I walk into the kitchen and he's standing at the table folding towels. He's not only done laundry, but he's cleaned the kitchen too and even has dinner going.

He has checked off everything on my to do list other than work on the painting I need to finish.

You did all this? I ask, shocked. I was ready to wake up and get it done before Liz got home.

Yes. Now let's have some lunch and then you can go paint. Sit down, he nods toward the opposite end of the table. Then after pulling everything out to make sandwiches, he makes us both one and gets some chips from the panty. He sets the plates on the table and gets us both a glass of water.

I've never felt so pampered in my life.

Thank you, I say as he sets the water down and then kisses the top of my head before sitting down with me to eat.

Once we are done, he is the first up to grab the plates and takes them to the sink.

When does Liz get home? he asks.

She takes the bus and gets dropped off at the driveway just after three fifteen.

*That is just over two hours away. Go paint, h*e says, kissing my temple and pushing me toward the third bedroom that I've turned into my studio.

Once in my studio, I sit in front of my current painting, but my mind starts racing. He's been here and in a few hours has helped out more than anyone else in my life. Yes, my mom has been over to visit and see Liz. But she hasn't lifted a finger to help. I get she is grieving the loss of a child, and not just any child, but her favorite child.

My dad took time and mowed my yard, but that was it. While it was helpful, I really need help inside.

So even though I should be painting, I sit, staring and process everything he's done for me. Finally, I start painting, getting lost in my art and tune everything out. So later, when Zane walks in, I jump.

Liz will be home in about twenty minutes. I thought you might want to clean up.

I look at the clock, shocked so much time has gone by.

Putting things away, I wash up and go to the living room where Zane is and walk right into his arms.

Thank you for today. I tell him.

I'd have been here sooner if I knew. He leans down to kiss me. But his lips aren't on mine for more than a second, before the front door bursts open and Liz walks in. When she sees Zane, she freezes.

I speak to her and sign so Zane is in the conversation too.

Liz, this is Zane. Zane, my niece, Liz. He came over to help me out today. He is deaf.

Picking right up, she signs as she talks.

Is he the one you wanted to learn sign language for?

Yes.

Very nice to meet you, Liz. I didn't know you knew sign, Zane says.

A girl in my after school class is deaf, and I wanted to be her friend so I learned."

I notice that Liz grins big at Zane. So far, so good. Then, she goes right to the kitchen, setting her stuff down at the table, she rifles through the kitchen cabinets.

She will have a snack then do her homework. I tell Zane before we walk into the kitchen.

Zane sits down next to Liz as she pulls out her homework.

What do you have for homework?

Math. I hate math, she sighs.

Well, it just so happens Math was my best subject, Zane says.

While he helps her with her homework, I finish making some sides and bread to go with dinner. Things have been very sad around here, but for the first time since my sister died I hear my niece giggle at something Zane said and it heals my heart just a little.

He's smiling and they seem to be getting along really well. I start to picture this as a regular thing, being able to have it every night. I want it so much my heart aches. But I also don't want to ever push Zane into a choice he may not have wanted.

He has admitted he didn't want kids and I couldn't live with myself if I changed his mind because he didn't want to lose me, but then later regretted it and walked away. I need to protect not just my heart, but now also Liz's.

Once she finishes her homework, she runs off to play in her room while I finish dinner.

She is a smart kid. Even though she doesn't like math, she is good at it, Zane says.

I think she is throwing herself into school since the accident.

Over dinner, we talk about her day at school and she asks more about me and Zane. In order to get to know each other better, Zane asks questions. Then he cleans up the kitchen while I join Liz in her room.

"What do you think of Zane?" I ask her once we are alone.

"I really like him. He looks at you like dad looks at Mom." Then she pauses and tears well up in her eyes. "Looked at Mom," she, bursts into tears.

I pull her into a hug and just let her cry. That is how Zane finds us later on. When he wraps us both up in a hug, that's what seems to be what helps her calm down.

I'm sorry, she says.

You don't ever have to be sorry for missing your parents. The love you have for them will never go away. You will always miss them, but you will learn how to cope. I've lost people in my life and I still miss them, but the sadness goes away and the memories keep them with me, Zane says.

"I agree baby. I miss them too. So much. It's still so new and it's going to hit you at the weirdest time. Lean into your grief. It's how we will heal. Eventually, it won't make you as sad when you think of them. But until then, it's perfectly normal and you don't ever have to apologize for it. Especially here." I sign while speaking.

Is it okay if I get ready for bed now? I'm really tired," she asks.

"Of course."

When she goes to take a shower, Zane and I sit in the living room.

Once on the couch, Zane pulls me into his arms like he knew I'd need his strength. And I do. I let my wall down because what she said hits me hard. Zane looks at me like Brian did to my sister. I always loved my sister's relationship. You could tell how much Brian loved her and I know that look because I saw it on his face so often.

To know I won't ever see him looking at my sister like that again, and to know I will never get to witness their silly flirting and see them sneak kisses when they think no one is looking, makes me sad and angry that their lives were cut so short.

I don't know how long we sit in each other's arms when Liz comes out to give me a hug and kiss before bed. But then she surprises us both and hugs Zane.

Will you be back tomorrow?

Do you want me to be?

She stops and thinks about it for a minute.

Yes, I like you being here.

I stay silent, waiting to see what Zane says. Though I couldn't agree more with her.

Then I will be here.

Liz smiles happily, and I'm happy that Liz feels the same as me.

Then it's time to get her tucked into bed. I decide to skip story time tonight because she is fighting to keep her eyes open.

When I get back to the living room, Zane is standing.

Noah is on his way. I don't want to leave but I have to. Do you want me to come back? he asks.

After Liz goes to school tomorrow, I will have Art Therapy at Oakside. Maybe you can come home with me after?

I'd love that. Also, can I get your number? He holds up a phone.

Taking it, I enter my name and number as the lights from Noah's car fill the driveway.

Zane leans in and kisses me. We both want that kiss to last longer, but we don't want to keep Noah waiting either.

Tomorrow. He says with a huge smile and I nod.

Yes, tomorrow will definitely change things.

CHAPTER 18

CARLEE

As I stand in my living room window and watch Zane and Noah leave, the house suddenly feels empty. With Zane here, I felt strong and everything hurt less to have him by my side, to know I wasn't alone in this. Now I'm back to having to be the strong one.

When I go to check in on Liz and peek my head in, I expect her to be asleep. So when I see her staring back at me, I almost jump.

"Is he the one you were telling Mom and Dad about?" she says barely above a whisper.

"Yeah he is," I say, walking into the room, leaving the lights off, and sitting on the edge of her bed.

"Did she ever meet him?"

Her voice is wobbly, so I reach out and take her hand.

"No, they didn't get to." I'm unable to keep the emotion from my voice.

"I think they would have liked him. I really like him," she says.

"So you wouldn't mind if he came around the house more?" I want to make sure because she has had so much change and upheaval.

"I know you had a life before all this, I heard you and Mommy talk and I don't expect you to put it on hold to raise me."

Hearing her words, something in me snaps into place.

When Liz was born, Kaylee was so worried about being a mom that she had no idea what to do, that she'd say the wrong things and screw the kid up for life. She would cry about it long into the night.

The day Liz was born I was standing next to her at the hospital and she said it was like the missing Mom piece of her snapped into place and she knew she could do it. Well, I think my sister just gave me her Mom piece because suddenly I feel it and know I can handle this.

I lie down next to Liz and pull her in my arms. She rests her head on my shoulder.

"I'm going to tell you something, but you can't tell Grandma and Grandpa. I haven't told them and now isn't the time to bring it up, okay?"

"I promise," she nods her head.

"Your mom and dad were planners. Long before you were born, they talked about their will and made plans for what would happen to you if they died. When they had you, I was in high school, so in their first draft of the will you would go to Grandma and Grandpa if anything happened."

"What changed?" she asks.

"Right after I turned eighteen, they asked me to come over. Even though they knew I had plans for school, they asked if anything were to happen, would I raise you. They said Grandma and Grandpa were getting older, along with a few other adult things."

"Like they didn't like how Grandma treats you."

The way she said it was not a question. This must be something she heard her parents talk about.

"Sometimes, you are too smart for you own good. Yes, like that and how Grandpa lets her do it. So they changed their wills and made sure that I was your guardian."

"And you said yes."

"Well, I had some questions first." I say wanting to be honest.

"Like what?"

"Well, what if I was still in college? They said Grandma and Grandpa could help. The big thing I was worried about was the money to raise you, since I was barely supporting myself. They said they would take care of it and make sure I had everything we'd need. After talking it out, I agreed. It was never that I didn't want you, it was I wanted to make sure I could take care of you."

"Do you have everything you need now?" she asks.

"Yes. But it leads to some questions I want you to think about, okay? They left me their house. It's paid off thanks to the inheritance your dad got when his grandpa died. So if you want, we can live there. I can sell this place or rent it out. I'm not sure yet. Both would give us money. Or if you want to stay here, we have to figure out what to do with the other house. They also left some money in savings which will take care of you. I am working part time and selling my paintings, but I'm going to look for something full time. We are okay with money, and I need you to know that."

"Would you be okay living in Mommy and Daddy's house? I feel closer to them there," she asks.

"It would be hard at first, but it's where they wanted you to grow up and I know they would love to see you living there," I tell her. "But don't make up your mind right now, just think about it."

"Okay," she says softly.

"Now for the big part that you can't tell Grandma and Grandpa. They knew all that, but this is what they don't know."

"What is it?"

"I can't have kids. Do you know that car accident I was in that everyone talks about?"

"Yeah, I don't know much, but I've heard everyone talking about it."

"When I was in the accident, a tree branch was lodged in my belly." I lift my shirt and show her my scars.

"They did emergency surgery, but to save my life, they had to remove my uterus. That's the part of me that would hold a baby. So I can't even have a kid. I want you to know that because I know you really wanted a little sister. But I also wanted kids more than anything. But getting to raise you is like getting my chance to be a mom. I know I will never replace your mom, and I'd give anything to have my sister back, but I want you here and I need you here too." I hug her tight.

"Grandma and Grandpa don't know you can't have kids?"

"No. It took me a bit to process and come to terms with it. I told your parents about it not too long ago. Oh, and Zane knows. I was working up the courage to tell Grandma and Grandpa. You know how much Grandma is pushing for me to find someone and give her more grand babies, so I guess I'm just scared of her reaction."

"Make sure Zane is there when you tell her. He will scare her into line," Liz giggles.

"They haven't met him yet either. Not that I'm hiding him, it's just there hasn't been an opportunity. I planned to introduce your parents to him when they got home. But I had already told your mom about him and she approved."

"Now you've told me too," she whispers.

"Well, I hope you know you can talk to me about anything. I don't want our relationship to change too much. We can still be friends, but now I have to deal with the not so fun stuff too." I tell her.

"I'd like that." She says around a yawn. "You know Mom and Dad would have loved Zane. I just know it."

Once again tonight, my eyes water and I fight back tears.

"I think so too." I say, hugging her and tucking her in to bed. Then I close the door, hoping she will have a good night's sleep.

Going to the living room, I pull open my laptop to check my email. There is so much to do with probate, lawyer's meeting, and the funeral. Brian's parents can't even make their own son's funeral, since my parents insisted their bodies be shipped here instead of us going up there.

It's been a mess and not something I want Liz to worry about. I know both of us are already dreading the funeral.

Part of me wishes we could fast forward over the next year. Then all of this will be settled and we can work on healing.

CHAPTER 19

ZANE

The last week has been something I never would have expected in a million years. I went to Carlee's sister and brother-in-law's funeral. Noah came with me to translate, and Lexi came to support Carlee. Most of Carlee's friends from Oakside were there. Beforehand, we agreed that to her parents I'd be a friend because this wasn't the time to get into it.

With everything in me, I hated it, but I still didn't leave her and Liz's side. Her parents paid her so little attention they didn't even notice me. Even though I get they are wrapped up in their grief, it's like they forgot they have another daughter who is now raising their granddaughter. It all just doesn't sit right with me, but Noah says we have to give them time. They have to process it.

Every day, I've been over to Carlee's place. She picks me up and Noah comes and gets me at night. Through all this, he and I have become good friends.

How is she really doing? Noah asks me as we pull into Carlee's driveway today. He gave me a ride because he had some other things to do in town.

She is handling it better than I expected her to. But I think there is a lot on her plate as well. She and Liz have talked a lot and are trying to figure out if they are going to stay here or move into her sister's house. If they do, then she'll have to figure out what she will do with this place. Her sister and brother-in-law were good with their money, so she isn't stressed on that end. It's her parents that are making her anxious. They ignore her, then show up and try to tell her what to do.

If she needs anything, she can let us know or you let us know. We have lawyers, mediators and more all at Oakside that would be willing to help her, Noah says.

I will let her know, I tell him as I get out of the car.

Walking to the door, I knock once before opening the door. Carlee told me to just come on in, but I still like to let her know I'm here.

I find her sitting on the floor with papers spread out on the coffee table and all around her.

What's wrong? I ask.

My mom showed up last night after you left. She questioned me over and over about if I really want to raise Liz and saying I'm too young to be trapped with the responsibility. The irony! I went off on her about how she is always pushing me to have kids, but now I'm too young to raise one. She just kept saying I have options, and no man wants to raise someone else's kid. When I finally kicked her out, Liz came to me crying after hearing the whole thing. It took me over an hour to calm her down and remind her how much I love her and want her.

I'm angry at myself that I wasn't there for her. I know I have to be at Oakside, but I should have been there for her too.

What does that have to do with all the papers? I ask, sitting down at the coffee table across from her.

I'm checking all my bases concerning the will and other papers from my sister. After last night, I felt unsettled, but I didn't want Liz to find me going through all this, so I waited until she left for school.

It all starts to click. This is why she called and asked Noah to bring me over today.

Noah wants me to remind you they have lawyers and all sorts of people who can help if you need it.

She sighs, flipping through a few more papers.

I might ask him if there is a lawyer to look through this. A second opinion, I think, might calm my nerves. Then she stacks all the papers up and puts them back in a folder.

He'd be more than happy to help. I tell her as I stand and move to the couch, pulling her on to my lap.

I want to talk to you about something, but if it's not a good time, it can wait.

No, please tell me. I need the distraction.

I've begun the process to transition out of Oakside. I don't want her to know how nervous it makes me, but at the same time I'm excited because it will give me more freedom to help her as needed.

What exactly does that mean?

Well, I guess it means I've healed enough that they think I can take care of myself. I'm working with my doctors to transition out of Oakside into the real world. They brought in Lexi's sister-in-law who is working to get me ready to do. I need to figure out what I'm going to do. Going back to school seems like a good option. I can do it all online. But for what I don't know. Another thing she'll do is help me find a place to live and get set up. I met with her today and she is getting some information together for me.

Do you have any thoughts on what you want to do?

Other than be here for you, not really. I always thought I'd be a lifer in the military, but that's not an option, so now I'm not sure. Tonight, I have some course curriculum books to read through and hopefully, maybe something will jump out.

Liz really like having you here.

I'm not quite sure where she is going with it, but my heart races, making me wonder if she can feel it.

Just Liz? I ask, trying to get her to keep talking.

Me too. Liz is doing so well with our routine and she's doing good in school. Her teachers are surprised how well she is coping with everything that's happened. I think that's because of you sitting down to do her homework with her every night. I like having you here. It makes me feel stronger, like the weight of this isn't crushing down on me.

I swear my heart stops and starts all over again. Just hearing she wants me here and that my being here isn't more of a burden on her is everything I could want. I wrap my hand around the back of her neck and pull her in for a kiss. Just a soft one that shows her how much that means to me. Transitioning out of Oakside is scary, but having her at my side is what is making me push through it.

Suddenly she pulls away. For a minute, I think maybe I misread it.

Someone is at the door, she says, standing.

I take a deep breath and will my cock to go down because he's ready for her anytime she is near me. Though I haven't made a move on her since she got the news about her sister, but he is more than ready to be inside her again with less than a moment's notice.

When she opens the door, her mom is there and pushes her way inside. She doesn't look the least bit happy to see me.

CHAPTER 20

CARLEE

"Mom?" I ask, shocked she is here.

"Who is he?" she says.

"This is Zane you met at the funeral," I say, signing at the same as talking, trying to make sure Zane is included in the conversation.

"Oh, he's that deaf one. Why is he here?" Her irritation is clear.

"He is here to support me. Why he is at *my house* is none of your business. Now, what do you want?"

"So this is how you spend your days with some guy instead of working?"

"It wasn't that long ago you were pushing me off on any guy who looked my way," I remind her. "Also, it's my day off, so I'm working on freelance projects. Now, what do you want?"

"I don't think men like him should be around Liz," my mom says.

I hold on to my temper by a thread.

"Men like what, Mom?"

"Broken, bad boys. You will never fix him. You should be focusing on Liz, but since she isn't your priority, you should know that your father and I are perfectly able to raise her."

"Yet we both know that isn't what Kaylee and Brian wanted because they didn't make you her guardian, they made me. When they changed the will when I turned eighteen, they made that perfectly clear in the will and letters that went with it."

"What they want doesn't matter so much as what is best for the child." Mom dismisses me.

"What is best for her is to be with someone who loves her, not someone who tears her down every chance she gets. She is thriving in school and we have a good working routine going. She has met with counselors, and I've met with her teachers. All have said she is doing better than they expected. I'm going to raise her. I am able to do it, and it was Kaylee's wish. How I do it is none of your business."

"It is so! She is my grandchild. I will not have you ruining her."

"Legally, she is my child, my responsibility, so no, you have zero say. Now, if this is how you are going to behave in my house, you can leave. I have things to do, and I'm done with you today. I don't have time for this." I push her toward the door.

"Well, I never!" she says, as I open the door for her.

"Well, bless your heart!" I say and close the door behind her, making sure to lock it. I'm abundantly thankful I never gave her a key.

Since I wasn't translating what my mom said, I turn to Zane, and give him a recap. His face says it all. Right now, he is starting to doubt himself and how important it is for me to have him here.

Stop. You being here is a good thing. Liz is thriving because of you. She told me how much she likes you and how much her mom and dad would have liked you. She wants you around. Because I wanted to be sure, I have asked her that several times. It's not only about Liz. I really want you here. I tell him, climbing back onto his lap, this time straddling him.

Kissing him with everything in me, I desperately want to finish the kiss that was interrupted. When he pulls back, I still see the worry in his eyes. But he attempts to distract me, and I let him.

Go work on your painting. I know you are close to finishing it. I will figure something out for dinner and get going on picking up around here.

The rest of the day, we fall into our routine, and it takes away the nerves my mother being here caused.

When Liz gets home, she is none the wiser to Mom's visit and her hurtful words. Though an idea has been circling around in my head all day, and I want to make sure it's okay before I talk to Zane tonight.

While Zane cleans up the kitchen, I help Liz get ready for bed, and like we have been every night, I lie down and talk to her.

"I want to ask you something, but I'm hesitant because there has been so much change in your life already," I start.

"If this is about Mom and Dad's house, I'm not sure yet. I want to live there, but I like it here too. I think moving in there will just make everything too real. But I don't want to sell it either," she says with way more insight than any six-year-old should have to have.

"You take your time with that. I want to ask you about Zane possibly moving in, even temporarily." When she answers, I'm glad, smart girl that she is, that she's been giving it some thought.

"I'd like that. When I get home from school, I'm happy he is here, and I like knowing he makes you happy. But why would it only be temporary?"

"Well, he is transitioning out of Oakside, and his life is about to have a lot of changes. There are many choices he will have to make. I don't want to pressure him and make him think he has to stay here. Though

I would love it if he did, but I want him to find himself and do what makes him happy, too," I tell her.

"You are what makes him happy, Aunt Carlee. I can see it all over his face and in his eyes."

At her words, my eyes tear up. Even though I want nothing more than for that to be true, I worry he won't be happy here long term. I don't share that worry with Liz because she has had so much change in her life she doesn't need to be anxious about anything else.

"My goal is making you happy, so I just wanted to check in," I tell her, unsure of what else to say.

"I'm okay right now. My therapist said it's all right that I won't be happy for a while," she says.

When she tells me that, I'm grateful the first thing I did was get her the therapist the school recommended. I knew she'd have a lot of emotions and thoughts, and I wanted to make sure she could process them all. I wanted her to have someone else to talk to as well.

"She's right. We will be happy. Though it might take a while. Now get some sleep," I kiss her forehead and tuck her into bed.

Once she is settled, I go to the kitchen and find Zane reading something on his phone. Walking up to him slowly, I don't want to startle him. As I get close, he looks up and smiles at me before standing, taking my hand, and leading me to the couch in the living room.

So Liz and I have been talking. I start once we are settled.

Should I be scared? He jokes with a smile on his face.

Well, I'm scared, but I hope it's a good scared.

His face goes serious, and he waits for me to get it out.

I've been thinking about how you said you are transitioning out of Oakside. Well, Liz and I have been discussing how much we really like you being around. Then, pausing I take a deep breath.

I'm not going anywhere, he says

Good. Because we were hoping you might think about moving in with us. I get it out and then sit there as he stares at me, instantly wishing I could take it back.

You want me to move in with you? he asks.

Yes, Liz does, too. She likes you here, and it was the first time I've seen her really smile when I asked her about it.

For a moment he doesn't say anything. Instead he looks out the front window even though it's almost dark outside. When he turns back around, happiness is written across his face.

I would love to live here with you two. More than anything.

So, is that a yes? I ask, as Noah pulls into the driveway.

Yes. I don't have much. Some boxes that were sent to Noah from my barracks.

We will make it work. There is a chance we will move into my sister's house, which is bigger. But we can talk about all that later.

I give him a quick kiss because we don't want to keep Noah waiting.

Even though this feels like a big deal and a big change, I'm ready for it.

CHAPTER 21

ZANE

What a change in the last few weeks. All my stuff has been moved over to Carlee's. Well, actually to her sister's house, since we decided our next move would be there. We had the conversation as a family, and I was honored to be a part of the discussion. We talked and decided the best choice was to rent out Carlee's house, which would give us some extra income. At least for now, it was the best course of action. Though we decided to watch the market and see when would be a good time to sell. That way if we could make some money on the sale of her house, we could put it in savings or use it to buy something else.

Another major plus is that her sister's house is paid off. Kaylee and Brian were really smart with their money and left Liz well taken care of.

Won't be many more days I have to drive you over here, Noah says as we pull into Carlee's sister's driveway.

I guess I could start thinking of it as my house, but I'm not quite there yet. My transitioning out of Oakside is going well and my doctors have signed off on everything. The biggest hold-up is I still don't know what I want to do, whether to go to school or get a job. It's great I have everything I need to live here, but after that, I'm not so sure.

They have set me up with translators when necessary, and I'm explor-ing my options.

Listen, now isn't the time to talk, but I'd like you to be with me in a meeting. There is someone coming to Oakside to tour the place. Her husband was military and killed in action, and I want to run some ideas by both of you, Noah says.

Okay, let me know when. When I get to the door, I knock, but then walk in. While I know there is no need to wait for her to answer the door, I still like to let her know I'm here. She normally greets me, but today she doesn't, so I go toward the back of the house and find her on the floor of the family room crying.

I rush over, thinking she hurt herself, but she keeps shaking her head.

I'm okay. She hands me the piece of paper in her hand.

I sit on the couch, pulling her up next to me, and tuck her into my side before reading the paper.

In short, her mom is suing her for custody of Liz and contesting the will her sister and Brian left. I didn't think this was possible, but the paper in front of me says otherwise. Because I know this could get tricky, Carlee is going to have to lawyer up.

Okay, we need to talk to Noah. He will have a good lawyer for you, is the first thing I say as I comfort her.

Grabbing my phone, I hope Noah will answer quickly. The sooner I can get a plan in place, the faster I can make her feel better.

> **Me:** Hey, do you have a good lawyer you can recommend? Carlee's mom is suing for custody of her niece.

Thankfully, Noah replies right away.

> **Noah:** Fuck. Yes, I know some good one. I'll send the info over in a few. Let us know what else you guys need, no matter how small.

I take a moment to soak in how easily he said anything we needed, they'd help us. How he knows this fight is mine as well as Carlee's and that we are fighting this together is all it takes to know I'm right where I need to be.

Baby, Noah is on it, and he's getting you the best lawyer. You aren't alone in this, I say.

I know. I just can't understand why she is doing this. Then she rests her head on my shoulder, as if to absorb my strength.

We sit like that for a while before she tenses and sits straight up.

What is it? I ask.

I'm going to go confront my mom. I need to know why she is doing this, and she is going to tell me to my face.

I don't think that's a good idea. I think we should wait and talk to the lawyer.

I know. That's why I need to do it before we get a lawyer. Once we do, there is no talking to her on my own. She is my mother, and she owes me at least this.

I can't object because I agree. Her mother does owe her this. Plus, I'm a might curious about what her parents are thinking.

Okay, let's go then. She looks at me, and I know what she is going to say before she says anything.

Me not going is not an option. I want to know what she says because I have a good idea it has to do with me. I will ask Noah to come translate. You know, having support is the best thing, and Noah needs to know what is going on.

She stops and thinks for a minute, nods and picks up her phone, calling Noah. They talk for a minute before she hangs up.

He is on his way over. He also agrees it is not a good idea but is coming anyway.

Good. Go get cleaned up. Your mother doesn't need to know you were crying and how much this has already affected you. Don't give her the upper hand.

She smiles, kisses my cheek, and runs upstairs. While she is gone, I text Noah.

> **Me:** I don't like the idea of her going over to her mother's.

> **Noah:** Me either, but with me there, I can at least make sure we have the details and form the best plan going forward. All of Oakside will be behind you two.

> **Me:** Thanks. See you soon.

I have to admit I'm choked up, knowing this man who I've known for such a small amount of time, is on my side and that so many people are rooting for me and ready to help. It's such a foreign, yet welcome feeling for me.

As soon as Noah shows up, I can tell he is concerned, but Carlee hugs him, and as much as I want to yank his hands off her, I know she needs comfort. The smirk on his face tells me he knows what I'm thinking.

I'm driving, let's go, he says.

We don't argue as I climb into the backseat with Carlee, pulling her back into my side once again. I hold her the entire way there, and I can tell she is inside her head, so I just let her think it all over. Because if I know her, and I do, she is rehearsing what she is planning to say.

As we pull into a house smaller than the one Carlee's sister left her, I start to wonder if this is more about money than Liz.

When we walk up to the door, her mom answers. The moment she sees us, her face dramatically changes. The warm and friendly face she had is gone, and the one left is cold and unwelcoming.

I have nothing to say. You can talk to my lawyer, Noah translates.

When her mother tries to shut the door, Carlee slams it back open. The shock is clear on her mom's face before she schools her features. Then, a side of my girl comes out I have never seen before.

• • • •• •• • ••

Carlee

She has nothing to say to me? Like hell she doesn't. If she isn't going to talk, I have plenty to say.

Making sure Noah is ready to translate, I lit into my mother.

"The least you can do is look at me, your only living child left, in the eye and tell me why you are doing this."

"Look at the poor choices you are making. A part-time job. Some old deaf guy? Really, Carlee?" Mom says.

"What is going on with all this noise?" Dad asks, coming to the door.

"Are you aware she is suing me for custody of Liz?" I ask. The look on his face says he wasn't, but I know he won't admit it.

"While you go through this rebellious time in your life, it's just better Liz lives with us. You can have your own kids one day," Mom says.

"Actually, I can't. To save my life, when I had the accident, they had to do a hysterectomy. I can't ever have children. And I was just hired full time at Oakside. I'll be doing art therapy, and they are paying for me to get some extra certifications. A nice bonus is the State will pay me even more money.

You have been so lost in your grief that your favorite child is gone, but you haven't given two shits about the one you have left. Now you have lost her too," I say.

Without giving her time to respond, I turn and march to Noah's car. Right behind me, having my back are Noah and Zane.

No one tries to say anything as Noah drives us back to my house. I'm grateful, but I know they will want to talk once we get there. The problem is, I don't know what to say. Other than I guess I need to talk to a lawyer.

My phone is going off like crazy. Since it's only texts, and if it was Liz's school, they would call if they needed me, I ignore it.

When we get home, Zane leads me back to the family room and pulls me into his lap, while Noah sits at the other end of the couch.

"I guess I will need the lawyer's info." I break the ice.

When my phone goes off again, I pull it out and find several texts from my mom.

> **Mom:** We just don't want you to be saddled with the responsibility of a child so young. What if the right guy is turned off by it?

> **Mom:** Liz needs a stable home, and having someone like Zane in it isn't stable.

> **Mom:** Besides, you have never raised a child. I could do it better.

I show the texts to Zane and then Noah.

Maybe I should leave if I'm the problem. Zane says, looking defeated.

Don't you dare. This is a time for you to stick together, not let her mom pull you apart, Noah says, glaring at Zane, but also driving a point home to me.

We are stronger together. Liz likes having you here, and she is used to you. There is no point in changing things up now and throwing her off. I tell him.

The last thing I need is for him to leave. Right now, he's the only thing keeping me together.

Sorry, I didn't tell you about the job. I just got the email today from Noah right before I got that letter. I tell Zane, not wanting him to think I'm keeping things from him.

It's great. I can tell you how much you like working there, he says, smiling.

Well, I should get going. I need to get that info for you, and the last thing you need is me here when Liz gets home to make her start asking questions, Noah says.

Let me walk you out, Zane says, standing after setting me gently on the couch.

Let me know if you need anything, Noah says.

I promise to keep him updated.

What a day. I knew my parents were distraught, but I thought as their grief faded, they would come around and be here for Liz and me. Boy, was I wrong.

CHAPTER 22

ZANE

When I walk Noah out to his car, he turns back to look at me.

What is it? he asks.

I don't want to leave Carlee alone tonight, not with all this going on. Is it possible to stay with her?

He pauses for a moment, and then a huge smile lights up his face.

Yeah, I was hoping you'd want to, but I didn't want to push you if you weren't ready. Having you around will be good for her. Just let me know if you need anything.

Noah gets in his car, and after he is gone, I still stand in the driveway, giving myself a few minutes to gather my thoughts.

When I go back inside, Carlee is on the couch where I left her. I hate that I let my doubts get the better of me and suggest that I leave. The second I said it, I regretted it.

Picking her up, I pull her into my lap and hold her tight to me. The stress of the day is evident in the tenseness of her body. Fortunately, she snuggles up against me, and relaxes with an audible breath. I love that I can be that safe place for her.

My dad didn't know that Mom was doing this. I could see it in his face, but he wouldn't contradict her in front of us. Though, I'm pretty sure they're having it out right now.

Come on, let's get you lunch. Liz is going to be home soon, and we need you in tip-top shape, so we don't worry her, I say, causing her to look at the clock.

Thankfully, she doesn't fight me. We make our way into the kitchen, and I make her a sandwich. Even though she's eating, it's obvious she's not herself and a million miles away.

As Liz walks in the door, Carlee ate the last bite of her sandwich. But she schools her features fast, so thankfully, Liz doesn't seem to notice as she comes bouncing into the kitchen and grabs a snack from the pantry. She waves a piece of paper in Carlee's face and has a huge smile on her face.

Carlee*Look straight A's,* Liz says.

Glancing over Carlee's shoulder, I see the report card in her hand and sure enough Liz has straight A's for the last quarter.

This is amazing. I am cooking you whatever you want for dinner tonight. I tell her.

Can it be baked mac and cheese? My mom always made me it when I got straight A's. It's my favorite.

When Liz's smile falters, I know she's thinking about her mother. But then she smiles again and walks over to the counter where there's a little plastic box. She opens it and starts flipping through the index cards before pulling one out.

This is her recipe, she says.

When she hands to me, I look it over, and see we have all the ingredients that we need.

I'll get started on it, and you think about what you want for dessert. I'm so proud of you.

In return, she gives me a big grin. Then she shocks me by walking over and giving me a hug.

We've gotten into a routine that works for us. Liz will sit down at the dining room table, pull out her homework, which, for the most part, is either math or her spelling words, and gets right to it.

After she finishes, and while I cook, she and Carlee talk.

Since she has been living with Carlee, Liz is thriving. Although she was a straight A student even before her parents' accident, the fact that she's been able to keep it up is a testament to Carlee's love and support. How her mom can think that she can't handle this is beyond me.

I make a note to plan for both of them to have a girls' day. Maybe go to the spa and get their nails done. Something fun. Carlee needs some stress relief, and Liz deserves it after working so hard. I think a little bonding time will do them both good. I'll have Noah ask Lexi for recommendations on places to go and make sure I set it up to give them a fun day.

After chatting with Carlee, Liz goes to the family room to watch one of her shows.

Before long, dinner is ready, and Lexi calls her to the table.

This tastes just like my mom's! Thank you, Zane, Liz says. Then she proceeds to stuff her mouth full of macaroni and cheese. I've never seen this girl eat so much. No surprise that after eating four large helpings, she groans about having a tummy ache.

That's what happens when you eat too much. You have to pace yourself. Let me get you some medicine, and then you can lie down on the couch for a little while before you get ready for bed, Carlee says.

While I work on cleaning up the kitchen, our night goes on like normal. Once Liz is in bed, Carlee joins me in the kitchen. She walks right up to me and hugs me as I wrap my arms around her. We stand there for a minute before I pick her up and set her on the kitchen counter so that she's almost at eye level with me.

With everything going on tonight, I really don't want to leave you alone, so I talked to Noah. As long as it's all right with you, he gave me the okay to spend the night. We can use it as a trial run. What do you think? I ask, holding my breath, waiting for her answer. She breaks out into the first genuine smile I've seen on her all day.

I would like that because I was not looking forward to being alone tonight either. But be warned, I am very used to sleeping on my own and I think I'm a bed hog.

Oh, I'm not worried about that. I plan on keeping my hands on you, so there will be more snuggling than bed-hogging going on. I lean in and kiss her.

Running my hands up her sides and back down to her hips, I'm enjoying the feel of her. I could stand here and kiss her all day, and that's a feeling that I have never had before with anyone.

When I'm about to end the kiss, she groans and wraps her legs around my waist, holding me to her.

Then, with a smile on my face, I pick her up and carry her to the bedroom.

• • • ● • ● • • •

I wake up to a hand stroking my face, and when I open my eyes, Carlee is there looking at me with a smile lighting up her eyes. For a moment, we stare at each other and I know without a doubt this is how I want to wake up every morning.

You said last night that you wanted to be up to help get Liz ready for school. My alarm just went off, so I thought I'd wake you up.

I don't know what their morning routine is. But I know with all my heart that I want to be a part of it. Just like I've been part of their evening routine.

Why don't you get ready and help get Liz up? While you're doing that, I will make some breakfast, I say.

Smiling, she nods her agreement, so we get up out of bed and face the day. After she wakes Liz up, I head to the kitchen. For breakfast, I decide to make some eggs and bacon to go with some of the leftovers from the night before last.

By the time Liz comes stumbling into the kitchen, dressed for school, she looks completely unhappy to be awake so early, not that I can blame her. When she sees me, she smiles big.

I like having you here for breakfast, she says.

Her words touch my heart, making me glad that I have her and Carlee.

I like being here, too, and being able to take care of both of you, I say as Carlee walks into the room.

Immediately, she pours herself a cup of coffee. *I'll eat after I get her off to the bus.*

We watch as Liz shovels food into her mouth. Though she's barely able to finish everything on her plate, before Carlee has to rush her off to be at the end of the driveway for the bus. As they go out the door, I start making our breakfast.

When she walks back in, I ask, *How do you like your bacon cooked?* I want to know everything I can about her so that I can make her breakfast without having to ask.

Limp, she says.

Excuse me? I ask, not sure that I read the sign right.

She smiles once again and says, *I like my bacon limp.*

At this point, she's laughing, and I stalk over to her letting out a growl.

That is the only thing that is going to be limp in this house, I say as I pick her up, tossing her over my shoulder and smacking her ass.

She knows exactly what she was doing. On the counter next to the stove, I keep one hand on her as I use the other to cook the bacon and eggs.

Noah sent me an email with the info for the lawyer that he suggested last night. I just saw it while I was checking my email this morning, she says as we're eating at the table.

Well, it looks like our next step is to go talk to the lawyer. She smiles for a minute, though I'm not quite sure why.

I was hoping you'd want to go with me. Noah volunteered to go as a translator for you. At least until we can get someone who can help out on a more regular basis.

There is nowhere else I'd rather be than by your side. I know it sounds cheesy, but it's the truth.

This woman is making me do and say things I never thought I would, and I wouldn't have it any other way.

CHAPTER 23

CARLEE

The shrill sound of the alarm goes off as if I need it to wake me up. Today of all days, I am wide awake before the sun is even up. Because today I meet with the lawyer to counter sue my mother.

What the actual fuck?

It's just so wrong that my own mom is suing me and that I have to counter sue. But there isn't a thing I wouldn't do for Liz. I swear that mother instinct kicked in because one look at her sweet face and I know I'd die for her without blinking an eye. I'd kill to protect her, and I'd spend every last penny I own to keep her safe and happy.

Even though I never want her to doubt that her life is stable, I'm not sure when to tell her about all this, either. Eventually, she's going to ask where Grandma and Grandpa are.

Turning over, I stare at Zane's sleeping form next to me. Having him here has been everything I needed. He's been my strength, my rock, and my voice of reason. He suggested we wait to tell Liz what's going on, until after we meet with the lawyer. That way, we'd have more information and an idea where things were heading.

I place my hand on the side of Zane's face and gently stroke his cheek. His eyes open and he smiles up at me. All the time he tells me this is his favorite way to wake up-me there with him. Though before we both roll out of bed, he pulls me in for a quick kiss. Our routine is pretty much set by now. While I get Liz ready for school, he gets breakfast going.

Last night he made biscuits, so Liz wanted bacon and egg biscuits for breakfast this morning. When she made her request, we both laughed, remembering our limp bacon conversation. She wasn't thrilled when we said it was an adult joke.

I go into Liz's room and turn on the lamp next to her bed, gently rubbing her back.

"Rise and shine," I say, softly.

It takes a minute, but Liz sits up in bed, yawning.

"Today is our ice cream party," she says, jumping out of bed.

Her class had the most books read in her entire school, so they are having an ice cream party to celebrate. She has been looking forward to it all week.

In record time, she's up and dressed and ready for school, sitting at the dining room table before I am.

She is really excited about the ice cream party. I think it's the fastest she has ever gotten ready. Zane says after handing me a cup of coffee.

During breakfast, Liz keeps asking if we are thinking they will have this kind of ice cream or that kind of ice cream. She promises to give us a play-by-play detailed description of the party when she gets home. Finally, it's time for her to go, and I watch as she skips down the driveway to the bus.

"Bye, Aunt Carlee!" She calls before climbing onto the bus.

I watch the bus leave, then go back inside where Zane has made our breakfast and is waiting for me at the table.

Like we do every morning, we have breakfast together and then get ready. Since Noah said he'd meet us there, we don't have to rush to the lawyer's office.

All morning Zane couldn't seem to keep his hands off of me, as if I'd disappear into thin air.

He's constantly touching me. Wrapping his arms around my waist as I brush my teeth. Brushing my hair for me and watching me braid it. Rubbing my back as I put on some makeup. Even going so far as to help me get dressed. Wherever and whenever he could, he was there.

In the car, he holds my hand the entire way there. When we get to the lawyer's office, Noah is waiting for us in the parking lot.

You guys ready for this? Noah asks.

Not really, but we don't really have a choice, do we? I say.

Zane wraps his hand around my waist and guides me into the lawyer's office.

Noah takes the lead, introducing us and explaining he's there to translate for Zane. Then, we are led back to the lawyer's office.

Before we sit down, all the same introductions are made.

"So, in short, I've gone over your sister's will and the paperwork your mother has filed. You have a strong case. How is Elizabeth doing in school?" Mr. Arwood, our lawyer, asks.

"She just brought home straight As. Today her class is celebrating reading the most books by having a party. In her class, she had the second most books read." I tell him.

"So, she is happy and well adjusted. Any acting out?" Mr. Arwood makes some notes.

"No none. We have routines in place for her. When she comes home from school, she has a snack and then does her homework. We continue to have family dinners, just like my sister used to do."

"And what is Zane's role in her life?" he asks.

"Every night, he helps her with her homework. Together, they have learned ASL, teaching me as well. He helps with meals and makes breakfast every morning before she goes to school."

"Well, we will need notes from her school about her grades and how she is coping. Also, it might help to have her talk to a court appointed therapist to prove she is doing well and is happy. It won't look good that your mother is using a man's disability against him. Especially, considering that all of Oakside is by his side. They are well known in the community and it's not a good look for your mother.

While we are waiting to see the judge, there should be no contact with them, outside communication between me and her lawyer. No visiting with Liz, no contact, nothing. Now, I just have a few standard questions."

My head is already spinning, and we've just started.

"Do either of you have a criminal background I should be aware of?" he asks.

"No," I tell him, and then look over at Zane.

He shakes his head no, too.

"Any health problems?" Mr. Arwood asks.

"No," I say.

Nothing except I'm deaf from war injuries. Zane says, while Noah translates.

"What about employment? Do you have a way to support the child outside the money Kaylee and Brian left you?" Mr. Arwood continues his questions.

"Yes, I have a house I just bought, and my job just went full time teaching art therapy at Oakside. They are also paying me to get some state certifications to teach a few more advanced classes."

"Currently, Zane is employed full time with Oakside. He's helping us with a project and is under Non-Disclosure Agreement at the moment." Noah says, still signing for Zane.

Zane is fast at hiding the surprise on his face, but I see it. It's a relief knowing Zane isn't keeping anything from me.

"All right. I think I have everything thing I need. If not, I'll get back to you. Today, I will be filing the notice that we plan to counter sue and let you know what their response is."

We say our goodbyes and head out.

I think now is the time we should tell Liz what is going on. Zane says once we are back in the car.

I agree. She will start to wonder why Grandma isn't even calling, I say.

The entire way home, I think about what I'm going to tell her and go over possible questions she might ask.

Once we arrive home, we have lunch and try to keep our minds off the conversation ahead.

What did Noah mean that you have a job with them? I ask as we sit in the living room.

He mentioned talking to someone and wanting me there, but that was it.

Our conversation is cut short when the school bus pulls up and I go meet Liz in the driveway.

As soon as Liz sees Zane standing in the living room, she drops her backpack. He never greets her like this and the worry etched on his face is visible, even to her.

What's wrong? She asks worriedly.

We need to tell you what is going on. It's adult stuff, but it affects you. I tell her as we all sit down on the couch.

I'm not sure how to explain this simply, but we won't be visiting Grandma for a while. She thinks she should be raising you despite what your mom and dad wanted. So, we have to let a judge decide. While we're waiting for that to happen, we can't go to your grandparents' place or even talk to them. I'm relieved to finally get it out in the open.

She looks between Zane and me and then crawls into Zane's lap.

He looks at me over her head as he wraps his arms around her and holds her tight, comforting her.

I want to stay here with you two. Can I just tell the judge that? She asks with tears in her eyes.

My eyes are watering too. *Oh, honey, I wish it was that easy.*

Yes, I wish all this was just as easy as a six-year-old makes it.

CHAPTER 24

ZANE

I'm on my way down to meet with Noah in his office. Ever since he told the lawyer I have a job, I've been anxious to hear what he has to say. I know without a doubt, he never would have said what he did about me working full time at Oakside without a plan.

When I get to his office, there is a man and woman I've never seen before sitting on the couch talking to Noah and Lexi.

Zane. Come on in and close the door. Let me introduce you to Storm and his wife, River. Their son Jason is back at the house with my sister, and we were talking about the kids. Noah says, filling me in on what I didn't hear when I walked into the room. I need to remember to tell him how much I appreciate his consideration.

River smiles at me and starts talking, but I look over at Noah, who is translating for me.

Storm was in the military with my husband and was his best friend. Right after we found out we were expecting, he was killed in action. We had some trouble, and it turned out to be a long battle, but I had Storm by my side through it all. In the end, he fulfilled the promise he made Jason to take care of me if anything happened to him.

Noah pauses, so I look over at River and Storm and they are smiling at each other with love in their eyes. I know there is a story, but it's not why I am sitting here, so if I get the chance later, I will have to ask them about it.

I know many surviving spouses of fallen military men and women don't have the support and help I did. Storm moved me to Whiskey River, Montana and his friends rallied around me, no questions asked. Now that I'm on my feet and our son is a bit older, I really want to help those spouses that are in the same boat I was. A friend of ours suggested reaching out to Noah here at Oakside, and he issued us an invitation.

Then she proceeds to offer me a job. Even though she answers all my questions, it actually leaves me with more. Thankfully, Noah takes over from there.

I want you to be in on this new service we'll provide at Oakside. You have the connections we need. We'd get you an assistant to take phone calls, but everything can be done by email, contracts, proposals, all of it. Anything that has to be done in person, we will provide you with a translator. It would allow you to work here with Carlee. You will have an office down the hall. The hours are flexible, so you can be there for Liz as needed, Noah says.

As I attempt to process it all, Noah continues.

You would work with Becky. She is bringing on a new girl to help with her workload and once she is trained, we are budgeted to bring on one more that will work directly with you and the spouses you are helping, Lexi says.

When I got the news my husband had been killed in action, I was given thirty days to get out of military housing, plan his funeral, and figure the rest if my life out. If it hadn't been for Storm, I don't know what I would have done. I had nowhere to go, River says.

I don't know if you know this, Lexi says, *but I was married to an Army guy before I met Noah. Tyler was also killed in action, and I too was given thirty days to make plans. But I was one of the more fortunate ones, as I was able to come back here with my parents and lean on them while I recovered. Becky was my biggest support. Without them, who knows where I'd be.*

I had no idea, I say. *Even though I know a few men who didn't make it home on deployments, I never knew what happened to their families. By the time I got home, they were gone. Noah* continues translating for me.

I want you to go home, think about the job and talk it over with Carlee. Don't give me an answer right now. I know everything you guys have going on and you have a lot of plans to make. But if you say yes, you would be involved in setting up this entire department and work with Becky on what you will need to do the job. River and Storm have donated some of the money we require to get this up and running. Also, Oakside has allocated a budget for this too. Mandy is working on grants and some fundraising as well. That means there will be some public events for you to speak at, Noah says.

Even though I want to say yes and jump at this opportunity, if I want to make a life with Carlee, and I do, then he's right I need to talk to her.

I'm definitely interested. Let me talk to Carlee tonight and get back to you. I tell him.

Holding his hand for me to stop, he pulls his phone out and frowns at it.

Zane, it looks like you have a visitor at the front desk. I will walk up with you, Noah says.

We say our goodbyes and leave.

Any idea who it is? I ask him on our way back to the lobby.

Carlee's dad, he says.

I stop in my tracks. *She isn't here today.*

I know. He's asking to talk to you. That's why I'm going. Not just to translate, but to be there as a witness to what's said.

Taking a deep breath, I walk into the lobby with Noah at my side.

I don't know if I should be relieved or on guard that he is alone, and Carlee's mom isn't there.

Can we talk? Her dad asks.

You know sign? I say, shocked.

I helped Liz learn it. It might be best to bring your friend with us, as I'm not great at it.

Noah leads us to the dining room and gets us lunch. We sit in a back corner and then he starts talking.

When I learned my wife was suing for custody, I was shocked. I went back and forth about telling you that, but I feel it's important. I don't know you and I want to since you mean something to my daughter and are around my granddaughter.

What do you want to know, sir? I ask, keeping it formal.

First, call me John. Second, I want to know where you came from, and your plans now that you are leaving Oakside. But most of all, I want to know if you can take care of my girls.

I grew up in North Carolina, but don't plan to go back. Because I didn't have a great relationship with my parents, I joined the military to get out of the way. I loved the military, and it suited me. After I became a SEAL, they became my family. I planned to do twenty or more years with them. But my injury derailed those plans.

As far as my future employment is concerned, Noah and I have been talking about me setting up and heading a new department here at Oakside. I need to iron out the details and discuss it with Carlee. But it would allow me to be flexible and be there for Carlee and Liz, I say.

Before I can say anymore, Noah chimes in. *We will be providing him with a translator for work, and he doesn't know it yet, but after this he is meeting with Paisley who trains the service dogs here at Oakside.*

We are getting him a hearing dog. Noah has a big grin on his face as he claps me on my back.

My jaw drops open. I didn't even know this was a thing. We hadn't talked about it.

I didn't know that was a possibility. I tell him.

Paisley reached out to some contacts and found a dog that was mostly trained when you transferred here. She finished the training, and he's now ready to work with you. I just heard from her this morning before our meeting, Noah says.

What would a hearing dog do? John asks.

Basically, the dog will alert him if the doorbell rings, if an alarm goes off, if the phone rings, if someone is calling his name, or if there is screaming. Paisley will work with the dog to let Zane know if something is wrong with Liz and a few other commands helpful for working around here. That is, if he takes the job, Noah says.

I can't be upset that there will be someone else looking out for my granddaughter, John says.

During the rest of lunch, he asks me questions about my life, like growing up, my military time, and other subjects that pop up. We talk for quite a while. He tells me some stories about Carlee, how she was as a child and teenager and some of her exploits. How he loved her painting and was happy she could use it in her career. All in all, we got along, and by the end, I'm thinking we're going to be friends.

Right now, I'm going to go home and talk to my wife. I'm going to be honest. While I love Liz, the thought of raising her full time is a little much. Since Carlee wants to and is much better suited to be her guardian, it should be her. I'd rather respect Kaylee's wishes. John he takes a moment to wipe his eyes as they tear up.

After I shake his hand, he leaves me standing there in the lobby dumbfounded.

If you have the time, I think I'm ready to head home. I have a lot to talk to Carlee about before Liz gets home from school, I say to Noah.

Let's go. Also, I set you up with a driving instructor who will go over some small changes you need to make. Then you'll be able to drive again, Noah says, grinning.

How can I not smile? Everything's coming together, and I owe so much to this man right here. I don't know if I will ever be able to repay him for his kindness and thoughtfulness. Someday I will have to try to express to him how much everything he's done means to me.

CHAPTER 25

CARLEE

Over the last week, Zane and I have gotten into a well-oiled routine. When Liz is at school, we spend our days at Oakside.

The day he came home and told me about Noah's proposal to work at Oakside, I could see the excitement all over his face.

It was a no brainer, and I told him to take it. But he still wanted to talk it out, so we did. He even went so far as to talk to Liz about it, and she was very excited for him. So, he accepted the job that night. He then got out a notebook and a pen and started jotting down all his ideas and questions.

He's still so excited about the job and enjoys what he's doing. One of the biggest perks of the job for him is that it allows him to still be here in the mornings for our routine of getting Liz off to school and having breakfast together. Then we go to work together, we get to come home together and be here to meet Liz when she gets off the school bus. Then he gets to help her with her homework, which she absolutely loves to do with him.

When he told me about his conversation with my dad, to say that I was shocked my dad showed up would be an understatement. I was even more surprised to learn that they got along so well. I thought maybe he was just saying that to cover for my dad, so I texted Noah since he had been there, and he confirmed it. Noah said he was just as shocked as I was.

Zane also started working with Paisley, who will train him for his hearing dog. Next week, he has his first driving class, which will give him even more freedom. Liz is super excited about Zane's hearing dog, especially once she learned she'll be allowed to take the dog outside and throw a ball around and play with him. She's always wanted a dog, but her dad was severely allergic.

We just wrapped up another day at Oakside. I am now teaching art therapy three days a week. The other two days I come to Oakside and have open art classes. Anyone can join them, patient or family, and even staff members have joined in. I'll be teaching how to draw certain landscape scenes, and will entertain requests on what they want to draw. According to my students, they have a blast in my classes. I have fun too.

As we pull into the driveway after another great day working together at Oakside, my phone rings. The caller's identity flashes across the car clearly displaying that it's the lawyer. Immediately, the tension that fills the car is unmistakable. My parents have been silent and so have the lawyers, so it's been easy to put it all out of our minds, forgetting the counter suit.

"Hello?" I answer hesitantly.

"Hello, Carlee? This is Mr. Arwood," he answers, and I translate for Zane.

"Yes, is everything okay?" I skip the pleasantries and want to get right to the point.

"I am calling you to give you an update. I had filed all our paperwork in preparation to go to court against your mother. But our office received a call yesterday that she was dropping the lawsuit and received the paperwork this morning. I want to just check with you before filing any paperwork with the court, as I'm assuming that you don't want to move forward with anything on your end," he says.

I sit there stunned.

"She dropped the lawsuit. All of it? The custody, contesting the will, everything?" I ask, needing to be sure.

"Yes, she claimed a change of heart," he says.

"Wow! Oh, okay, yes, I would love to just be done with this. What are your suggestions for moving forward?" I ask.

"Right now, we're in good shape. I needed to know your thoughts before I could proceed. I will file the paperwork with the court that we agreed to end this, and that's it. If you need me again for anything, I'm here," he says.

"Will I be getting an invoice via e-mail?" I need to know the amount in order to work on our budget for the month.

"Oakside has covered the bill, so you won't receive any invoice. All the billing has gone directly to them," he says.

We say our goodbyes, both of sitting in the car surprised and grateful.

Noah took care of our lawyer's bill. Zane asks just to clarify.

Seems like it. I say, still in shock.

Right away, he pulls out his phone and sends a text in the group chat between him, me, and Noah.

> **Zane:** Did you really take care of our lawyer's bill?

> **Noah:** Yes, we did. It's part of the services that we handle here while you are a patient.

> **Me:** But I was the one being sued, not Zane.

Noah: Small detail. You're an employee here, part of the family. We take care of the family. And Mr. Arwood gives us a good deal on his fees because we keep him busy with contracts.

Me: Thank you.

I'm barely able to type it out because the relief that hits me causes tears to fall faster than I can stop them. A moment later, Zane opens my car door, pulls me out of the car and into his arms. Bending down, he picks me up, carrying me bridal style into the house and into the living room, where he sits down and holds me in his lap.

While he lets me cry and get it all out, he rubs my back and holds me tight. Every now and then, he'll kiss the top of my head. When I finally feel like I can't cry anymore, I wipe my eyes and look up at him.

Before I get a chance to say anything, the front door slams.

"Aunt Carlee?" Liz calls out.

"Living room," I call back.

Liz is home. I tell Zane and try to pull away, but he doesn't let me.

Liz finds us on the couch together, takes one look at my face, and her smile falters.

It's good news this time, Zane tells her and holds his arm out for her to come sit next to him.

Grandma dropped the lawsuit. She's not going to fight us for custody, and she isn't challenging your mom and dad's will. When I tell her this, I can see she's relieved.

Exuberantly, she wraps Zane up in a hug, and he wraps his other arm around her, holding us both to him. We sit like that soaking up our togetherness and relief. One big happy family. It's always in the back of my mind how Zane had said he had never planned to be a father.

But every day, he shows us over and over again by his behavior this is where he wants to be. Yes, he said the words, but his actions have shown me otherwise.

Alright, let's get going on those spelling words, Zane says.

Laughing with both relief and sheer happiness, we all get moving. Zane helps Liz with her spelling words and her homework as I get dinner going. We all settle into our nightly routine. Just as I put dinner in the oven, my phone rings. It's sitting on the counter, and Zane and I both see from the caller ID that it's my mom.

I'm going to take this outside, I say.

He nods, understanding that I don't want Liz to hear whatever my mom has to say.

Stepping out onto the back porch, I answer the phone with no emotion in my voice.

"Hello," I say, waiting to hear what she has to say. If she notices the lack of reaction in my voice, she ignores it.

"Hello, sweetheart. We want to invite you over for dinner this weekend. It's been so long since we've seen our granddaughter." Mom asks me this in a perfectly chipper voice as if nothing has happened.

I pause for a moment before I respond, so I don't let my emotions lead.

"Why would I bring her over there after you tried to take her away from me? You tried telling me I wasn't good enough to raise her. That Zane wasn't good enough to be around her. So why would *we* want to be around *you?*"

There's silence on the other end of the line for just a moment before she speaks again.

"That's all water under the bridge now. We're family," she says sounding defeated. I almost feel sorry for her.

"You tried to sue me for custody against your daughter's wishes. What part of that describes family? I will protect Liz with my life, but that also means that I have to trust the people that are around her and I do not trust you to not try to take her from me again. At least not right now. And as long as we're being open and honest, you should know that Liz knows what you did," I tell her.

She lets out a gasp, and I can hear my father shuffling to the phone in the background. "Why would you tell her? She is just a child and does not need to be concerned about adult matters," Mom says.

"I told her because we knew she was going to ask why you weren't around, or why she couldn't talk to you or see you. It directly affected her, and that's why we told her. When she heard your plans, she asked the court if she could just tell them that she wanted to stay and live with me. Did you ever think or consider her feelings in all of this?" I ask.

"She's the only connection we have left to your sister," Mom says with real, emotion in her voice for the first time.

"I get that, but what do you think Kaylee's reaction would have been if she found out you were suing me for custody of her daughter after she had explicitly stated that she wanted me to raise her child?" While I know asking her that is playing dirty, but she has yet to apologize for any of it.

There's some shuffling, and then my dad's voice fills the phone.

"I will talk to your mom. Maybe we can start with phone calls until Liz is ready to see us, but throughout it all, I will make sure that your mom respects her wishes," Dad says.

"Thank you. I will talk to Liz and when she is ready, I'll set up a phone call with you guys. Not a video call, just a regular call. We'll work our way up," I say.

"Agreed. I'll talk to you soon," Dad says, as we end the call.

Everything okay? Zane asks, standing behind Liz so she doesn't see.

Might as well get this over with.

Hey baby, that was Grandma on the phone. They miss you and want to see you. I start, but she interrupts me.

No, I don't want to see them.

I figured, and I told them that. How about we start with a phone call? Zane and I can sit right next to you, and you can hang up whenever you want. You will be in total control.

She thinks about it for a minute before nodding. *I can do that.*

All right, head upstairs and wash up for dinner. I tell her.

Once she's upstairs, I turn to Zane.

Mom thought I was going to just let her have visits with Liz like normal after she tried to take her away from me. I tell him not quite sure how I feel.

We'll take it one step at a time, he says.

That one simple word, 'We'll,' showing that we're in this together, means more to me than anything he could have said. It's really nice to have someone to lean on right now.

CHAPTER 26

ZANE

Today, Carlee and I finished our day early at Oakside. There's a lot of work to do to get my new department set up, but I'm loving every minute of it. Noah actually listens to what I have to say and takes my ideas and runs with them.

Did you notice Noah was a bit more cranky than normal today? I ask Carlee.

We're lying in the backyard in the grass, enjoying the warmth of the sun. When I made an offhanded comment about how I miss our times sitting in the grass getting to know each other, she dragged me out here and we have been cuddling under the cloudless Georgia sky.

I did, and I asked Lexi about it. Apparently, he found out that his sister Lucy is dating someone, but she refuses to tell him who it is. She told Lexi that she met him at Oakside. Any idea who it is? I ask.

No, and neither do Noah or Lexi, which has caused Noah to go around all day giving the evil eye to any single male on the property. It's actually been kind of funny, she says.

How old is his sister? I ask.

She's twenty and going to school down in Savannah. But she's staying with Lexi and Noah and doing some volunteer work at Oakside on the side.

His sister technically is an adult, so I do get that protective side of him. Though it did not really come out in me until I met Liz. If the situation was reversed and it was Liz with some guy, I would probably be acting the same way Noah was.

You can't blame the poor guy, though. Noah just wants to make sure that whoever it is doesn't hurt his sister.

Oh, I don't blame him. I just think it's hilarious the lengths that Lucy has gone to keep the identity from them. Other people are talking about it, and no one has seen her with anyone. Obviously, she's really good at keeping it a secret. The whole staff is kind of impressed, she says, smiling.

We lay there for a bit more and my thoughts keep going back to those first few days of us sitting in the grass together.

Thank you for sitting out here with me. I really missed our times of just being, sitting beside you and getting to know you, I say.

It has been a while since we've been out on the grass, hasn't it? Things have changed a lot too, she says.

Well, the biggest change is now I can wrap my arms around you and hold you anytime I want. Even on that first day, I wanted to do that so badly it hurt. Fighting not to touch you was one of the hardest parts of being around you. I admit.

I agree. I think the next biggest change is I'm completely okay with not having any more kids because I feel like I was meant to raise Liz. She's my family. Even though I may not have given birth to her, I know that she's the child I'm meant to have. Of course, I'd give anything for my sister to be here, but she did give me the greatest gift of trusting me with her daughter.

Well, the biggest change for me is that you and Liz have given me the family I never dared to dream of and the one that now I could never imagine my life without. You two have accepted me for who I truly am, and I've never fit more into a family than I have with the both of you. Rolling over to my side, I look down at her so she can see exactly how much I mean every word I say.

Her eyes study mine for a moment before I sit up and pull the black velvet box from my pocket. My nerves are certainly in full force because I've been thinking about this moment over and over again for the last week or more.

I want you and this family more than I've ever wanted anything. I want to be your husband, the person that you lean on when you need someone. I want many more days like this just soaking in the sun. I want all the days of working beside you at Oakside or wherever life takes us. I want to be there for Liz, to be the one helping with her homework and making breakfast every day. I want to be the one going around glaring at all the single guys when she tells me that she's dating someone. And if you both will let me, I want to adopt her. I already talked to her, and she's more than excited and praying that you'll say yes to my next question. Will you marry me?

Holding my breath, I wait anxiously. Last night, when I asked Liz how she would feel if I asked Carlee to marry me, I was nervous. Liz was so beyond excited that I feared Carlee would notice. Right then, I knew that I had to ask soon because Liz would not be able to keep that secret much longer. Maybe that was the push that I needed to ask her today.

I'm hoping she'll say yes, and it looks like the tears in her eyes are happy ones. When she sits up, my heart jumps to my throat.

Yes, she says, nodding her head right before throwing her arms around my neck and holding me tight.

She just agreed to marry me, and it takes a moment for it to set in. We are going to make this family official. I'm going to be part of a family, something I didn't realize I wanted or needed so badly.

Epilogue

Zane

Several Months Later

I'm sitting at my desk in my office at Oakside and Liz is sitting on the couch that Noah put in specifically for her. She has been coming here after school to do homework, as things have gotten busier for me. Getting this new department up off the ground has taken quite a bit of work.

She loves it here, especially since my hearing dog, Radar, is snuggled on the couch beside her. I'm reviewing a budget proposal that a prospective donor had asked for when Radar jumps off the couch, comes over and nudges me alerting me of a noise. Then he goes and sits in my office doorway facing the hallway.

Stay here please, I tell Liz.

I walk up and find Noah and Jake in what looks like a very heated discussion in the hallway. Carlee is walking up on the other side of them, having just finished her daily art class. Thankfully, she walks to my side and starts translating.

Noah just found out that Jake's brother, Caden, has been writing to his sister during his deployment. Jake admitted to seeing Lucy and Caden talking, but didn't realize it went any further than that. Noah is wanting Jake to talk to his brother because he doesn't want his sister mixed up in a military relationship and Jake is saying no because it is their choice, and he is going to stay out of it.

Isn't Jake's brother Caden the one that Jake's wife dated before she and Jake got together? I ask, trying to put everything together.

Yep, he was the one here visiting last year before his deployment. He found out about Jake and Kassi by walking in on them kissing or cuddling or something along those lines. It was right as I started here not too long before we met, Carlee says.

Shaking my head, I turn around and head back to my office. I will let the two of them figure it out because that seems like it's more of a family issue than an outside staff issue.

I sit back down at my desk and pull my wife onto my lap. Once she said yes, we all decided that we didn't want to wait long to make our family official. After having a simple ceremony here in the gardens of Oakside, we opted out of a honeymoon. Instead, we took a weekend to ourselves, and Liz stayed with Noah and Lexi. Then we took a week-long family vacation to Disney World, paid for surprisingly by Carlee's parents as a way to apologize for everything they had put us through.

Now, Liz doesn't mind going over there for family dinners, but she still doesn't want to be alone with them. They respect her wishes and don't complain. They accepted me into the family, and her dad has been the biggest help, coming over to the house and showing me how to fix things or take care of whatever needs it.

A newlywed couple rented out Carlee's house, and they have been taking excellent care of it.

Best of all, both girls wanted me to adopt Liz, so the day after we were married, we filed the paperwork with the help of Mr. Arwood. He said that it could be done in as little as three months, which means we should be hearing about a court date any day now.

I'm ready to head home whenever you are, Carlee says.

I glance over the budget one more time, hit send to the donor, and stand to gather my things. When we get out to the hallway, neither Noah nor Jake is there anymore. Radar knows the way to the parking lot and leads us as my wife holds one hand and Liz holds the other.

Noah has become a good friend of mine, and often we'll sit and talk during lunch. I asked him one day what his plans had been for when he got out of the military if things had gone the way he thought they would. He said he would have married someone who didn't love him, and would probably end up being divorced. Possibly he would have kids that he might never get to see. The thought of where his life would be if he hadn't had his accident was something that he didn't like to think about.

He told me that his accident brought him Lexi, and the life that they have together is the one he never knew he wanted. Every day he told me he's excited to get up, hold his wife, love his kids, help support his family, and work here at Oakside.

I know that feeling because I wake up and think about how happy I am with the life I have. Had he told me that before I met Carlee, I would have thought he was sappy and honestly, pussy whipped. But I guess it's one of those things you don't understand until it happens to you.

These people are the greatest blessing of my life, and I wouldn't be here if a life-changing injury hadn't derailed my plans and put me right where I needed to be.

• • • ● • ● • • •

Want a bit more of Zane and Carlee? **Grab the Bonus Epilogue by joining my Newsletter** https://www.kacirose.com/Zane-Bonus

Want Caden and Lucy's Story? Grab it in **Saving Caden.**

https://www.kacirose.com/Saving-Caden

River and Storm's Story can be found in **Take Me To The Edge.**

https://www.kacirose.com/TakeMeToTheEdge

ALSO

Jake and Kassi's Story can be found in **Saving Jake.**

https://www.kacirose.com/Saving-Jake

OTHER BOOKS BY KACI ROSE

See all of Kaci Rose's Books

Mountain Men of Whiskey River

Take Me To The River – Axel and Emelie

Take Me To The Cabin – Pheonix and Jenna

Take Me To The Lake – Cash and Hope

Taken by The Mountain Man - Cole and Jana

Take Me To The Mountain – Bennett and Willow

Take Me To The Cliff – Jack and Sage

Take Me To The Edge – Storm and River

Take Me To The Valley

Oakside Military Heroes Series

Saving Noah – Lexi and Noah

Saving Easton – Easton and Paisley

Saving Teddy – Teddy and Mia

Saving Levi – Levi and Mandy

Saving Gavin – Gavin and Lauren

Saving Logan – Logan and Faith

Saving Zane – Zane and Carlee

Oakside Shorts

Saving Mason - Mason and Paige

Saving Ethan – Bri and Ethan

Saving Jake – Jake and Kassi
Saving Caden – Caden and Lucy

Club Red – Short Stories

Daddy's Dare – Knox and Summer

Sold to my Ex's Dad - Evan and Jana

Jingling His Bells – Zion and Emma

Watching You – Ella, Brooks, Connor, and Finn

Club Red: Chicago

Elusive Dom - Carter and Gemma

Forbidden Dom – Gage and Sky

Mountain Men of Mustang Mountain
(Series Written with Dylann Crush and Eve London)
February is for Ford – Ford and Luna
April is For Asher – Asher and Jenna
June is for Jensen – Jensen and Courtney
August is for Ace – Ace and Everly
October is for Owen – Owen and Kennedy
December is for Dean – Dean and Holly

Mustang Mountain Riders
(Series Written with Eve London)
February's Ride With Bear – Bear and Emerson
April's Ride With Stone – Stone and Addy
June's Ride With Lightning
August's Ride With Arrow
October's Ride With Atlas
December's Ride With Scar

Chasing the Sun Duet

Sunrise – Kade and Lin

Sunset – Jasper and Brynn

Rock Stars of Nashville

She's Still The One – Dallas and Austin

Accidental Series

Accidental Sugar Daddy – Owen and Ellie

The Billionaire's Accidental Nanny - Mari and Dalton

The Italian Mafia Princesses

Midnight Rose - Ruby and Orlando

Blood Red Rose – Aria and Matteo

Standalone Books

Texting Titan - Denver and Avery

Stay With Me Now – David and Ivy

Committed Cowboy – Whiskey Run Cowboys

Stalking His Obsession - Dakota and Grant

Falling in Love on Route 66 - Weston and Rory

Stalked By The Rebel – Chance and Jessa

CONNECT WITH KACI ROSE

Website

Kaci Rose's Book Shop

Facebook

Kaci Rose Reader's Facebook Group

TikTok

Instagram

Goodreads

Book Bub

Join Kaci Rose's VIP List (Newsletter)

About Kaci Rose

Kaci Rose writes steamy contemporary romances mostly set in small towns. She grew up in Florida but now lives in a cabin in the mountains of East Tennessee.

She is a mom to five kids, a rescue dog who is scared of his own shadow, an energetic young German Shepherd who is still in training, a sleepy old hound who adopted her, and a reluctant indoor cat. Kaci loves to travel, and her goal is to visit all 50 states before she turns 50. She has 17 more to go, mostly in the Midwest and on the West Coast!

She also writes steamy cowboy romances as Kaci M. Rose.

PLEASE LEAVE A REVIEW!

I love to hear from my readers! Please **head over to your favorite store and leave a review** of what you thought of this book! Reviews also appreciated on BookBub and Goodreads!

Made in the USA
Columbia, SC
23 September 2024

42861009R00089